DEATH ON THE SEINE

A Paris Booksellers Mystery

EVAN HIRST

Copyright

Death on the Seine is a work of fiction. Names, characters, organizations, places, events, and incidents are either products of the author's imagination or are used fictitiously.

No part of this book may be reproduced, or stored in a retrieval system or transmitted in any form by any means electronic, mechanical, recording, photocopying, or otherwise without express written permission of the publisher.

ABOUT THE AUTHOR

Spurred on by a passion for history and a love of adventure, Evan Hirst is an award-winning screen writer who has lived and worked all over the world and now lives in Paris.

Evan's *Paris Booksellers Mysteries* plunge into the joys and tribulations of living in Paris, where food, wine and crime make life worth living... along with a book or two.

She also writes the *Isa Floris* thrillers that blend together far-flung locations, ancient mysteries and fast-paced action in an intriguing mix of fact and fiction aimed at keeping you on the edge of your seat.

Find out more about Evan Hirst's books at

www.evanhirst.com

CHAPTER 1

Some days were good. Some days were great. And then there was the rarest day of all -- the perfect day.

For Ava Sext, it was a perfect day.

It was a beautiful day in May.

The sky was blue, the birds were singing and pale green shoots were appearing on the barren branches of the silver-barked trees that lined the Seine River.

Most importantly of all, this perfect day was taking place in Paris.

Smiling broadly, Ava strode down the rue des Saints-Pères on Paris's left bank. Spine straight, head high, she breathed in deeply, content to be basking in the early morning sunshine. In any city of the world, people would be delighted by the weather. But in Paris, a city of grey skies and rain-swept monuments, a beautiful day in May was so unexpected that both Parisians and tourists, as startled, as they were ecstatic, were out in force.

It was only 9 A.M., but the streets were already full of people rollerblading, biking, walking, jogging, or, this being Paris, the city of love, walking hand in hand.

While not in love, no one was more ecstatic than Ava as she hurried to the Quai Malaquais that overlooked the Seine River, for she was going to paradise.

She had only lived in Paris for six months, but her past life was already a distant memory. She had exchanged London's dark skies and rainy days for Paris's dark skies and rainy days... But anyone who knew anything would tell you that they weren't the same. Parisian dark skies were infinitely more poetic. If Ava were a painter, she would pull out an easel and a palette of blacks and grays to capture Paris on one of those poetic rainy days. But she wasn't a painter. She would have to leave that to someone else.

Passing by an upscale antique store, Ava slowed and studied her Parisian "look" in its large plate glass window. Living in Paris had not only changed the way she felt and thought... she often found herself feeling French at the oddest times. It had also changed her external appearance. Her colorful, quirky London style had given way to a more polished look.

Today, she was dressed in her new uniform of slim

black jeans and a well-cut white T-shirt. A green leopard print scarf snaked around her neck. Her long, shiny dark hair was pushed behind her ears. Her heart-shaped face was makeup free except for a touch of mascara and bright red lipstick.

In the six months she had been in France, the "must-wear" lipstick color had gone from a gothic-looking purplish black over the Christmas holidays to a pale barely-there touch of pink in early spring, only to come crashing back to the bright fire-engine red color that Ava now had on her lips. As she eyed the tall 27-year-old reed-thin woman who stared back at her from the store window, she had to admit she looked very "chic".

With a smile of approval, she turned, crossed the street and hurried down it, slowing only when she passed by Café Zola. On its outside terrace, a waiter in his forties was setting up tables for the inevitable crowd that would soon appear on such a glorious day. He was wearing a white shirt, black vest and a long, old-fashioned white apron -- the uniform of a traditional Paris waiter,

"Morning, Gerard," Ava said with a light wave.

Gerard lifted his eyebrows in gruff recognition of the pretty woman passing by but continued to place silverware on the tables without a word.

Unperturbed by his silence, Ava continued on her way.

The famous Parisian reserve had taken some getting used to. In London, people were always willing to chat or give their opinion to complete strangers. Whereas the French had an odd habit of speaking when you least expected it and not speaking when you did.

It made no sense at all to Ava. But some things just were. "*C'est la vie*," as the French would say... That's life.

Looking left to see if any cars were coming down the one-way street, Ava stepped off the sidewalk and headed to the pedestrian island, lost in her thoughts about life in France.

A tinny ringing sound pulled her from her reverie.

Her inner survival instinct told her to jump. As she leapt forward, a cyclist raced by, going the wrong way down the one-way street. Shaken, she stood up, brushed herself off and watched him ride away.

Several pithy insults were on the tip of her tongue, but she stopped herself. It was an exceptionally beautiful day. Paradise was a few steps away. Why ruin it by screaming at a madman on a bike?

Be generous. Be loving... she repeated in a mantra that was definitely not Ava-like.

But this was Paris in May.

It was time for change. It was time for a new Ava.

She slowed next to the gigantic marble statue of a woman with a sword that stood on a triangle of land between the two sides of the street. She eyed it. The woman was an allegory of the French Republic. She and her sword were announcing to the world that they were ready for anything.

Ava frowned.

Maybe she needed what the statue had... that very definite "don't mess with me" attitude. Would the cyclist have rung his bell and tried to mow the statue down if it had suddenly come to life and crossed the street?

Of course not.

The statue would have beheaded the cyclist with one swift swing of her sword.

Cheered by the thought, Ava looked right and left before crossing the next street, a busy thoroughfare. She bolted across car lanes, bus lanes and bike lanes to reach her destination: the 8.60 meters of bottle-green wooden boxes that were perched on a stone wall overlooking the Seine River below.

Paradise.

With a double twist of her key, Ava unlocked the heavy metal padlocks that secured the bottle-green boxes, one by one. When she unlocked the last lock, she flung the wooden tops back revealing rows and rows of used books in French and English.

She ran her hands over their bindings and closed her

eyes, then breathed in deeply. It was a ritual she had performed every morning since the green boxes had become hers.

The books in the boxes had a special odor that came from being stored next to the Seine. Ava liked to imagine that it was a secret scent made up of all the places that the passing boats on the river below had been to and the adventures they had had. Just as she liked to believe that in the past six months she had learned to like adventure, at least a little…

After all, she was now living in Paris.

Her gaze turned to the license taped inside the first green box. The license was written in French and had several official stamps on it. It stated that the city of Paris authorized Ava Sext to run this little part of paradise.

Ava was a "*bouquinist*": a bookseller that sold used books out of the green boxes that lined the Seine River in the center of Paris. Since 1859, concessions to the boxes that ran from the Pont Marie to the Quai de Louvre and from the Quai de la Tournelle to the Quai Voltaire had been granted by the city of Paris to a lucky few.

Ava grabbed a green and white striped folding lawn chair off the top of the books, carried it over to a tall tree and unfolded it. If the green boxes were her kingdom, her folding chair was the throne from which she reigned. From it, she could see the Tuileries Garden and the Louvre Museum on the opposite bank. Further down the river, the tall spires of a cathedral soared high in the air. Like Quasimodo, Ava saw Notre Dame every day, and she didn't even have to ring any bells to do so.

If she leaned against the stone wall behind her stand, she could watch the *"Bateaux Mouches"*, the flat-bottomed glass-topped tourist boats, drift by on the water below as they made their runs up and down the river.

She wasn't exaggerating when she told people that she worked in paradise.

Her book stand was paradise... paradise on earth.

Humming a cheerful tune that she made up as she went along, she hung a vintage rock concert poster on the stone wall, unfolded a rickety metal postcard stand and stood it up. She put a piece of folded paper under one of its wobbly legs to stabilize it. She then strung copies of turn-of-the-century engravings across the top of her stand. They made paradise look very colorful indeed.

Last of all, she rearranged the small assortment of bric-a-brac that her stand sold, items that the French and tourists loved as much as the books. This morning, there were two black cat vases, a set of souvenir cups from the south of France, a metal cobra candlestick that looked like it had come from an Arab bazaar in North Africa and a pair of blue porcelain rabbit salt and pepper shakers.

Ava picked the rabbits up and held one in each hand. "I'll be sad to see you two leave," she told them. Unsurprisingly, the rabbits remained silent.

For a brief instant, she thought of keeping them for herself. However, she put them back with regret as she remembered the first rule of a *"bouquiniste"*: Once something was in your stand, you sold it... No exceptions.

Not ready to see the rabbits leave, she moved the pair to the back of the box and hid them behind a cracked crystal ball.

With a sense of contentment that mirrored the sunlight dancing off the river below, she stepped back and gazed approvingly at her stand.

It was now officially open and ready for business.

It was a perfect day in paradise… A day where everything would go according to some celestial plan. A day where nothing could possibly go wrong. However, even Ava, with her over-active imagination, couldn't have imagined that she would meet a dead man before lunch and that he would walk away.

CHAPTER 2

Sitting in the shade of a tall tree in her green and white striped lawn chair, Ava turned the pages of her book as she studied the people strolling down the quay.

She sighed with contentment.

Hemingway was right. Paris was a feast for the eyes.

Tourists strode past wearing the universal tourist uniform of jeans and sports shoes. Most had their eyes glued to their phones as they checked their mail or took selfies. Elegantly attired salespeople from the expensive shops across the road strolled to the wall overlooking the river to smoke a cigarette on their break. There were even several Parisian women in black jeans, white T-shirts and some variation of Ava's leopard scarf that strolled by.

"How's the book?" a deep voice asked, pulling Ava from her people watching.

Recognizing the voice, Ava gazed up at the tall tousled-haired man hovering over her. "I have no idea, Ali. I'm just watching the show."

Ali Beltran, a trim man in his early-thirties who wore heavy black rimmed glasses that made him look serious and hid the wicked sense of humor he was known for, ran the book stand next to Ava's with his twin brother, Hassan. Ali was also a prize-winning painter who had graduated from the prestigious Paris school of arts, the Beaux-Arts Academy. The school was just up the quay from their stands.

"You do know that to the people going by you are the show... *Glamorous Paris bookseller hard at work*," Ali said with a grin.

"Thanks for the glamorous but hardly working is more like it. Maybe it's the weather. People are too happy to buy books." Ava glanced over at Ali's stand. It was open and ready for business. "I didn't see you arrive."

"I waved, but you were lost in your thoughts."

Ava eyed Henri DeAth's stand further down the quay.

It was also open.

Henri, a distinguished silver-haired man in his sixties, was deep in discussion with two Japanese tourists. Ava wouldn't be surprised if the three were speaking Japanese. There was a breadth and depth to Henri's knowledge that never ceased to amaze her. He was also an astonishing fountain of information on human nature and its quirks.

"Do you want to see Hassan's new finds?" Ali asked.

"More junk?" Ava joked as she rose to her feet.

"Junk?" Ali raised his eyebrows in mock outrage. "Hassan would never speak to you again if he heard that."

Ava followed him to his stand, curious to see what his brother had brought back from his latest trip. Hassan criss-crossed France buying the objects that she and other booksellers sold.

Ali and Hassan's stand was dedicated to art books. As Ava had discovered, each stand along the quay was different and reflected its owner's interests. Ava's stand was a mix of books in French and English. You might find a *Guide Bleu* to Paris from 1920 or a Harold Robbins potboiler from the 1970s.

At first, Ava had been puzzled that Ali worked at the stand. He was a well-known painter with gallery representation in Paris and London.

When Ava had asked him why a successful painter would want to spend time selling books on the Seine, he had waved his hand at the view.

"Look at what I see… Not to mention, the hundreds of people who go past. Alone in their studios, painters go crazy. They drink too much, get depressed and lose their inspiration. Don't forget Van Gogh and his ear. Being on the quay, I soak in enough inspiration for several lifetimes."

When they reached his stand, Ava peered into the large box of wrapped items on the ground.

"What treasures did Hassan find this time?"

"We'll soon see," Ali said as he unwrapped an item.

It was a music box. A picture of Buckingham Palace was painted on it. He wound its metal handle. The box played "God Save the Queen".

Ava burst out laughing. "That's so horrible, it's wonderful."

"Thirty euros?" Ali asked.

"Thirty euros?" Ava eyed the music box, astonished. "The corner's cracked."

"You're right," Ali said with a quick nod. He wrote "€35" on a sticker and put it on the music box. "The crack means that it's an antique," he said in response to Ava's look of reproach.

He removed a thermos from his stand and held it up. "Coffee?"

"I thought you'd never ask," Ava replied, taking two hand-painted porcelain mugs from the stand. "Your coffee is better than Café Zolas."

"If Gerard hears that, he'll banish you for life," Ali responded with a chuckle as he poured the coffee.

Ava glanced to her right. Henri was now speaking to a

man who was tattooed from head to foot. The two were examining one of Henri's books.

"I didn't see Henri arrive," Ava said.

"He arrived when I did," Ali answered. "You were deep into…"

"Paradise," Ava said with a smile as she sipped her coffee.

If Ava was here in paradise, it was due to Henri DeAth, her late uncle, Charles Sext, and her unlucky love life.

Six months earlier, her life had revolved around her job as a communication specialist in a boutique PR agency in London. In reality, boutique agency meant that she and her co-worker did everything as only three people worked there, and her boss's life was devoted to dining with the agency's clients. As her co-worker knew little to nothing about social media, Ava was stuck with the job of keeping their clients' social media posts running 24/7, with the help of an ever-changing team of overworked interns who quit as soon as they realized what the work entailed.

Her boss was not above joking to visiting clients about the unfortunate connotation that her last name had taken on. Ava couldn't count the times she had heard him say, "Ava's our little sexter."

That had annoyed her immensely.

However, she was born a Sext and had no intention

of changing her last name.

Her job would have been enough to send anyone over the deep end, but Ava was resilient and tenacious. She was determined to stay at the agency and work her way up, whatever that meant. But when Simon her boyfriend, a TV writer, announced he was moving to Bolivia to find himself and that this journey of self-discovery had no place for her, Ava had exploded in a mix of anger, sorrow and vodka. She had spent the next twelve hours sending out incoherent drunken tweets on behalf of her clients.

Sadly, no one even noticed that there was something odd about the tweets. That was the final straw. Ava quit her job. Before she could decide what to do, her uncle, Charles Sext, died in Paris.

Charles Sext, an eternal bachelor and avid collector of books, had spent a great part of his life at Scotland Yard as a detective. Upon inheriting money, he immediately quit the Yard and moved to Paris. There, through a series of chance encounters, which included meeting Henri DeAth, he became a bookseller on the Seine.

Curious as to how Charles could move from crime to books, Ava had questioned him on this at a family event.

"Crime is a light into people's souls. I've never considered myself a solver of crimes but a student of human nature. At Scotland Yard, I studied the worst kind. As a bookseller, I am continuing my exploration of mankind. This time, I do it from a lawn chair on the Seine after a good lunch and a glass or two of excellent Bordeaux. And I'm happy to say that that most book buyers are a better sort than murderers."

Charles created a trust in which he left Ava his apartment in Paris and a monthly stipend, on the condition she move there for a year. More than money, Charles had left her a philosophy:

My dearest Ava,

Do not grieve for me. I've lived a hell of a life… In fact, I have no doubt that might be where I'll be spending the rest of my days. I'm offering you the chance to take time to discover life while you're still young enough to enjoy it. If you come to Paris for one year, the apartment is yours. I'm sure Henri will find a way for you to take over my stand. I'm also leaving you a stipend so you have enough money to enjoy Parisian life.

PS. Take care of Henri for me and keep him out of trouble.

In a certain sense, Ava had inherited Henri DeAth when she inherited the apartment, although she was sure that he saw it differently.

Henri had been a French *notaire*, a notary. In France, a notary belonged to a powerful caste. They were wealthy, secretive and protective of their privileges, which went back hundreds of years. A notary was an agent of the state, appointed by the French Minister of Justice. A notary drew up authenticated acts from property sales to wills. Once he applied his seal to them, the acts had the legal status of a final judgment.

Henri had once joked to Ava, "Not only do we know where the bodies are buried, we buried them... If we didn't kill them ourselves."

A French notary giving up his practice before he was in his dotage or dead was a rare as snow in August...

Impossible.

Henri was that rare snow in August. But then Henri was an unusual man.

He had come to Paris as a notary to deal with a tricky inheritance. Charles's apartment and the country house in the middle of Paris where Henri now lived had sprung from that, as had the book stands and Henri's retirement. At a mere 60-years-old, Henri sold his practice to a nephew, moved to Paris and never looked back. That didn't mean his former clients didn't appear on a regular basis asking for advice that only Henri could give them. But after a long leisurely lunch at the Café Zola, they would leave, reassured.

Henri and Charles had initially bonded over their eclectic interests and talents. Henri's last name, DeAth, was

Flemish. *De* meant from. *Ath* was a city in Belgium. Over time, the pronunciation of DeAth had come to rhyme with the English word 'death'. As both men possessed a wicked sense of humor, Ava suspected that their last names made a long-lasting friendship inevitable.

"Sext and DeAth. Now that's a team," Ava's Uncle Charles had often said.

Before Charles's long-expected death from cancer, Sext and DeAth had gained a modest reputation for solving crimes. When an Italian countess disappeared, the two men found her in a week without the newspapers getting wind of the story.

The stolen Picasso? It had taken Sext and DeAth less than twenty-four hours to find the thief and the painting.

Those cases and others had led to a certain renown for the pair.

And now Sext and DeAth meant Ava Sext and Henri DeAth.

However, since Ava knew next to nothing about detective work, bookselling would have to do.

Hearing loud laughter coming from Henri's stand, she looked up. Henri and the tattooed man were doubled over in hysterics.

This confirmed what she had often thought... No one's name less suited them than Henri's did. Henri DeAth was life itself.

"You're an Aquarius, aren't you?" Ali asked as he continued to unwrap objects.

"Yes. Why?" Ava responded, savoring the rich nutty flavor of her coffee.

"You're going to meet a tall dark-haired stranger and…." Ali's voice trailed off.

"And what?" Ava asked, bewildered.

"I have no idea," Ali replied. "The rest is missing."

Ava glanced up and saw he was reading from a fragment of a newspaper page that seconds before had been wrapped around the glass ornament in his other hand.

"Here. See for yourself," Ali said, handing her the ripped piece of newspaper.

Ava read the horoscope, frowning. She noted the date. "The paper's two years old, and it's from March."

"Details!" Ali protested. "It's a horoscope for an Aquarius. You're an Aquarius. That's synchronicity."

Synchronicity was one of Ali's favorite concepts. It was a situation where two unrelated events become meaningful because they occur at the same time.

"A tall dark-haired stranger… That's pretty vague," Ava said, unconvinced.

"What more do you want, his weight and height?" Ali

asked. "You might be on the verge of meeting the love of your life!"

Ava sighed. Since arriving in Paris, her romantic life had been checkered to say the least. In the last few weeks, Henri and Ali had taken it upon themselves to help her, much to her dismay.

"What is it with you French and romance?" Ava asked.

"The last I heard, the population of London was almost nine million. Love had something to do with that."

Ava's face bristled with annoyance.

"Sorry. I'm only trying to help," Ali protested.

Ava handed the ripped piece of newspaper back to him." Here. I won't be needing it."

Ali shook his head. "Keep it. I'm not an Aquarius."

Ava poured herself more coffee, strode back to her stand and settled into her lawn chair. Looking over at Henri, she saw that he was now happily talking to a group of teens on skateboards. She glanced one last time at her horoscope, crumpled it up and stuffed it in the pocket of her jeans.

There was nothing wrong with being alone.

In her case, the company was excellent.

Glancing up from her book, Ava eyed the sun. From its position in the sky, she guessed it was noon. She had spent the morning reading her book or not reading it, as everything and anything had conspired to distract her. Customers had streamed to her stand non-stop, full of questions. She had sold ten books. Someone had even bought the cracked crystal ball. When a man had asked her the price of the rabbit salt and pepper shakers, she looked so distraught that he put them back in her stand and skedaddled off.

Forcing herself to concentrate, Ava read another half a page before glancing up at her stand.

And there he was.

Just as her horoscope had predicted, a tall dark-haired stranger was standing at one of her green-boxes with his back to her.

From behind, he was trim. He was wearing a long-sleeved navy blue shirt, jeans and sports shoes with red socks. The red socks were the detail that struck her. Anyone who wore red socks was either a dashing individualist, worked in fashion or was colorblind.

Ava had always considered horoscopes silly. Perhaps, she had been wrong.

Swiping on more red lipstick, she was about to get up and go speak with him when he turned. The man striking-looking. He had grey eyes and a candid smile. He was also in his fifties or sixties.

Obviously, he was not the same tall dark-haired

stranger that her horoscope had predicted. Ava had nothing against older men. It was just she saw herself with someone her own age, give or take a few years.

Studying him, she realized that his face was vaguely familiar.

He had the look of a "familiar stranger".

Just as Ali lived and died for synchronicity, Ava was fascinated by the concept of "familiar strangers".

Familiar strangers were people you saw over and over again, without you knowing them or them knowing you. Yet at any moment, your lives might intersect in amazing and unexpected ways. But until then, familiar strangers remained strangers. They were extras in your life, there to provide the backdrop for everything else.

Ava sighed, disappointed.

Right now, she had too many extras in her life. What she needed was a leading man.

She observed the man more closely. There was something odd about his behavior that she couldn't put her finger on. But since she'd had the stand, she had learned that human behavior was more vast and complex than she ever could have imagined. Her Uncle Charles had been right about that.

When the man began studying her permit, Ava's brain snapped to, in a burst of lucidity.

21

The man was a book stand inspector from the city of Paris!

France was a country of regulations. Henri had warned her about that. He had also said that in France regulations were meant to be broken... Just don't get caught.

Ava eyed her stand. The many ways it broke the rules jumped out at her. The postcard stand blocked the sidewalk. A Rolling Stones's concert poster was taped to the stone wall. That certainly broke some rule. She might even have too many knick-knacks, as their number was regulated.

Ava glanced at the statue of the woman with her sword. Inspired, she stood up, bold and unafraid. She took a deep breath.

It was time to go to war.

Throwing her green leopard scarf over her shoulder, she strode over to the man. "Can I help you?"

"I'm just browsing," he said. He continued to look through the books.

As casually as possible, Ava moved sideways and inched her postcard stand in until it was no longer blocking the sidewalk. She eyed the poster taped to the wall. There was no way she could remove it without attracting the man's attention.

A thought struck her.

Maybe the man wasn't a city inspector.

Maybe he was a book thief.

That would explain why he was looking around nervously. Still, he didn't seem like the type of man who would steal a copy of *Valley of the Dolls* or a vintage *Guide Bleu*.

The man moved to her second box and began to flip through the books. His eyes darted left and right as if looking for something.

Ava hovered nearby, watching him. She wasn't an expert on clothing, but the man's clothing looked expensive.

He Uncle Charles had often told her, "Never judge a book by its cover." But he had also said, "Clothes make the man." That only showed that maxims were more trouble than they were worth.

Regardless of his attire, the man was acting strangely.

Ava astonished herself by walking over to him again.

It was time to take the bull by the horns.

This was so unlike her that she froze, startled by this amazing transformation of her psyche.

Sensing her presence, the man looked up.

"If you're looking for something special, I can help you," Ava said.

The man smiled. This time, his smile was warm and full of charm. "I'm looking for Mr. Sext."

Ava caught her breath.

That explained everything.

23

The man didn't know that that her uncle was dead.

"I'm Ava Sext. His niece. Charles Sext's niece," Ava said, babbling. There was something hypnotic about the man's glance that was completely destabilizing. If she were a murderer, she would have confessed on the spot.

The man waited, silent.

Swallowing, Ava blurted out, "My uncle died last year. Is there anything I could help you with?"

The expression on the man's face changed. For an instant, he appeared completely lost. He took a few steps to leave and stopped, turning back to her.

"I have an issue I'm dealing with. Someone told me that Mr. Sext and Mr. DeAth could help me. But if Mr. Sext is dead, then Mr. DeAth is…."

"Right over there," Ava said, pointing at Henri who was now speaking to a woman with a bulldog.

"That's wonderful," the man said with relief. "I'll wait here till he's free." He began browsing through her books again. "I'm sorry about your uncle," he added, looking up.

"We all are," Ava responded.

She walked back to her lawn chair, sat down and picked up her book.

The man continued to browse through her stand, glancing at Henri every few seconds.

Why didn't he just walk up to Henri? Ava wondered as

she peered at the man over the top of her book.

It might be out of politeness. Or maybe he didn't want anyone to hear what he had to say.

With that, Ava closed her book.

The man had a secret.

He had to have a secret.

Tall dark-haired strangers by their very nature had secrets.

And if he was a book thief, he had chosen the wrong stand. Some of the other booksellers had valuable books, but Ava's highest-priced book was thirty euros.

As Henri continued his conversation with the woman with the bulldog, the dark-haired man became more and more agitated. It was almost as if he were afraid.

Suddenly, there was a loud roar.

A large motorcycle jumped up on the sidewalk from the street and came barreling down toward Ava's stand. The motorcyclist was dressed in black leather. The visor on his helmet hid his face.

When he saw the motorcycle, the man panicked. He ran off. Without hesitating, he dashed into traffic and zigzagged between cars. Some slammed on their brakes. Others honked. The man fell against the hood of a small red sports car. He righted himself, jumped onto the pedestrian island, dashed past the statue of the woman and disappeared down the rue de Seine.

The motorcycle didn't follow him. It continued down the sidewalk, jumping onto the street near Henri. It raced away in traffic. Ava tried to get its license plate number, but it was covered in mud.

Too upset to speak, she waved at Ali. However, his head was bent over his sketchbook. Forcing herself to act, Ava ran toward Henri. He and the woman were staring in the direction the man had run off in.

"Henri. Someone tried to kill that man," Ava said in a whisper, barely able to articulate.

"Who?" Henri asked, stepping away from the woman.

"The tall dark-haired stranger from my horoscope."

Henri eyed Ava, concerned. "Are you OK, Ava?"

In shock, Ava opened her mouth to speak, but nothing came out.

How was it possible that on one of the most beautiful days of the year, someone had tried to kill a man in paradise?

Another thought struck her.

She forced herself to speak. "Henri, the man's life is in danger. We have to help him."

Henri looked in the direction the man had run off in and then checked his watch. "There's nothing we can do now. I suggest we meet in half an hour for lunch to discuss it."

"Lunch! A man's life is at stake, Henri!"

"Do you have any specific idea where he is or how we can help him?" Henri asked, always practical.

Having no answer to Henri's questions, Ava conceded defeat. "I'll meet you at Café Zola in half an hour."

She walked back to her stand. Plunging her hand into her pocket, she took out the crumpled horoscope. She clutched the wrinkled paper as proof of what had just taken place.

For some reason, the tall dark-haired stranger had entered her life needing help, and she vowed to give it to him.

CHAPTER 3

Ava checked the time on her cell phone. It was exactly thirty seconds since she had last looked. Glancing at Henri, she saw that he was chatting with a new customer as if nothing had happened. She wanted to throttle him.

Ava might not be a detective or a notary, but she knew an attempted murder when she saw one.

She caught her breath as another thought occurred to her.

If the murderer had succeeded, she would have been in danger as a witness to the crime.

She might even be in danger now as she was the last person to have seen the man, a man, who at this very moment, might be dead.

To vanish that disquieting thought, Ava flogged her

goods shamelessly. To her astonishment, she made three sales in a row, including to her infinite regret, the rabbit salt and pepper shakers. Not one of her customers had tried to bargain her down. A first!

At exactly five to one, Henri closed his stand. Ava left her stand open. Ali would watch it.

When she had asked him earlier if he had seen the motorcycle drive down the sidewalk, he had said no. He had been busy sketching. Ava was disappointed, so disappointed that she didn't mention the appearance of the tall dark-haired stranger from her horoscope. In any case, while the man was a tall dark-haired stranger, she doubted that he was the tall dark-haired stranger from her horoscope unless horoscopes went around predicting murders.

Her mind racing, Ava crossed the street carefully. If the motorcycle was lurking nearby, she had no intention of getting run over.

When she entered Café Zola, Henri was standing at the zinc-topped bar speaking with Gerard. The café was crowded. It was the usual mix of tourists, locals, antique dealers and sales people from the nearby luxury shops.

"Our table's ready," Henry announced when he saw her.

Walking calmly before Ava, as if an attempted murder on such a beautiful day was normal, Henri maneuvered his way to his usual table. It was a white-clothed table set for four in a quiet back corner.

A reserved sign was on it.

Following in his wake, Ava wondered how Henri could be so cavalier when an attempted murder had taken place just thirty minutes earlier. Ever the gentlemen, Henri pulled a chair out for her. He then sat down across from her, pushing the reserved sign away.

"Henri," Ava said. She stopped speaking when she saw he was studying the chalkboard with the daily specials written on it.

Her Uncle Charles had once told her that to solve a case you needed to take it step by step.

First things first...

In the present circumstances that meant lunch, as it was one o'clock.

At exactly one o'clock every day that Henri was on the quay, come rain or shine, he would have lunch at Café Zola at "his table". Often, he would lunch with people he had just met at his stand. Other times, he ate with old friends who had stopped by to see him. Ava often joined them. She marveled at how his quiet charm put people at ease and drew them out. Moreover, he was sincere. He truly liked people, and they liked him.

Hadn't he told her that the secret of being a successful

notary was listening to people?

Sitting across from him, Ava wished he would order. If she didn't tell him her story soon, she would explode.

Gerard appeared with a bottle of Bordeaux wine from a small producer and poured a glass for Henri and Ava.

Henri sipped it and nodded. "What does Alain recommend for lunch?"

Alain was the chef. He owned the café with his cousin Gerard. Alain had changed Ava's relationship with food. The first time she had eaten lunch with Henri, she had ordered a sandwich. Alain, a tall thin man who was perpetually peering over the top of his glasses, was so upset that he had come out of the kitchen to see what was wrong.

The sandwich has been replaced by a *coq au vin*, rooster in wine sauce, and a *tarte tatin*, a caramelized upside down apple tart, for dessert. It was delicious. It was also life changing.

Ava's sandwich days were behind her.

"Grilled sole with capers, lemon and parsley, baby roasted potatoes and a green salad," Gerard answered.

Henri eyed Ava. "Is that OK with you?"

"It's perfect," Ava said. It sounded so tasty that it almost made her forget her tall dark-haired stranger.

Gerard jotted down their order and strode off.

Henri took another sip of his wine. No swirling or

sniffing for him. The wines he drank were simple and to the point. He beamed, content with the contents of his glass. Henri took another sip and looked at Ava. "Now, tell me the story."

Ava opened her mouth to speak and stopped. "I don't know where to begin."

"Start with the tall dark-haired stranger," Henri said. "The one from your horoscope."

Ava ignored Henri's amused look. "Of course, I first noticed the man because of my horoscope. But the newspaper was two years old and from March and we're in May... So the man couldn't have anything to do with my horoscope."

"Why don't you start at the beginning?" Henri asked, ever patient.

Ava took a deep breath and plunged into what had happened. She began with Ali and her horoscope, and then moved to the man's arrival at her stand, his suspicious behavior and his asking to see Mr. Sext. She finished with his being chased and nearly killed by someone on a motorcycle. She deliberately skipped over her believing that he might be the man from her horoscope as it wasn't really germane to the story.

Henri raised his eyebrows. "You're sure the man asked for Mr. Sext and not Charles?"

Ava thought back to her encounter. "He asked for Mr. Sext. Is that important?"

"That means he'd never met your uncle. Your uncle insisted that people call him Charles."

"He also asked about you. But he had no idea who you were even though you were at the next stand," Ava added, proud of her budding detective skills, skills that were not needed in the communication agency she had worked for. Ava continued, adding little details that she had noticed, like the man's red socks.

Henri smiled. "You're a chip off the old block. Your uncle would be proud."

Ava winced. Her uncle would have gotten the man's name, and he would have learned why the man had come in five seconds. Her Uncle Charles might even have jumped on the motorcycle and wrestled the rider to the ground, solving the whole case.

Gerard arrived with their lunch and placed it in front of them.

There were two perfectly grilled soles with lemon, capers and parsley and mouthwatering baby potatoes that looked so good you wanted to pop them in your mouth whole. A basket full of pieces of a crispy *baguette*, made by one of France's best artisan bakers, was also on the table.

For one brief moment, Ava forgot about the man and

concentrated on the feast in front of her.

Who knows? At that very moment, the man might be in another café, celebrating his escape from death with a hearty lunch. The French took their food seriously.

"Why did you notice him at the beginning?" Henri asked.

"From the back, he was a tall and dark-haired."

Henri's fork hovered over his plate. "The one from your horoscope?"

"You can laugh. My horoscope was right. A tall dark-haired stranger did come to my stand." Defensive, she took the piece of paper from her pocket and handed the crumpled horoscope to him. "He just wasn't the right tall dark-haired stranger."

Henri sipped his wine. "I'm a firm believer in signs, although signs only mean what you think they mean."

"You're saying that if I hadn't believed a tall dark-haired stranger would appear, the man wouldn't have come to my stand?"

"Only partly," Henri replied, taking a piece of bread.

"I didn't conjure him up. I'm not the sort of woman who conjures men up," Ava said, indignant.

Henri burst out laughing. "I didn't say you were. What did he look like, other than tall and dark-haired?"

Ava gazed around the café. Description had never

been her strong point. She pointed to a tall woman at the bar.

"The same height as that woman there," she whispered.

"1 meter 85," Henri estimated.

"1 meter 85," Ava repeated. "The man was simply dressed, but his clothes hung well. They looked expensive like his watch. He was also very charming."

"Charming?"

"Not seductive charming, just charming. There was something charismatic about him," Ava said.

"So a tall dark-haired man with charisma comes to your stand, and you let him get away?"

"He was in his sixties," Ava protested.

"Past his prime," Henri said, serious.

Ava winced. Henri was in his sixties.

"I didn't mean that," Ava replied. "He might have been older or younger. Age is hard to guess."

Henri smiled in agreement. "Some people are old before their time. Others remain young no matter what their age."

Ava had no doubt that Henri would remain among the latter.

No sooner had they finished their fish than Gerard appeared. He whisked away the dishes and brought them dessert.

Three months ago, Ava would have protested that she didn't eat dessert. But today, she knew protesting would be useless.

As Ava bit into her *crème brûlée*, a warm custard dessert topped with a layer of caramel, she could almost feel herself melting from pleasure.

"When he asked for Mr. Sext and Mr. Death, did he give you any idea why?" Henri asked.

Ava turned bright red. She should have started with that. "He said he had a question on a situation he was dealing with, and someone had recommended Sext and DeAth."

"No more than that?"

"No. The longer you talked with the woman with the bulldog, the more nervous he became. He kept browsing through the books, as if to calm him nerves. For a moment, I even thought he was there to steal something."

Henri cocked his head oddly.

"As for the motorcycle, he couldn't have seen it until it jumped onto the sidewalk. But he felt the danger long before it appeared," Ava said.

"He expected it," Henri replied.

"Once the motorcycle was on the sidewalk, everything happened so quickly. He dashed into traffic, fell onto the hood of a car, jumped off it and then disappeared down the rue de Seine.

"Did the motorcycle try and chase him?"

"No. But traffic had come to a halt. Cars were honking. It couldn't have chased him even if it wanted to."

"I saw him arrive at your stand and wondered why he was lingering so long," Henri said.

"Can't you ask your friends at the Quai des Orfévres for help," Ava asked. Quai des Orfévres was the former headquarters of the Paris Criminal Police, located down the river from their stands. Even though the Criminal Police had moved to the 17th arrondissement, people still referred to its headquarters as the Quai des Orfévres.

Henri shook his head. "I can't tell them that a man whose identity I don't know was almost run over for some unknown reason by a motorcycle that was driven by a driver whose identity I also don't know. That doesn't give them much to work with."

"What are we going to do?" Ava asked.

Henri appeared surprised by her question. "Order coffee." Henri turned and signaled to Gerard, raising two fingers in the air.

Ava lowered her voice and leaned toward Henri. "There's one more thing."

Hearing the gravity in her voice, Henri eyed her.

"I've seen the man before."

"Where?"

"I don't know yet," Ava said with a determined look on her face. "But I soon will."

CHAPTER 4

A loud roar echoed through the dark night, shattering the silence. Startled, Ava spun around. A large black motorcycle was racing down the deserted Quai Malaquais toward her. When the dark-helmeted driver gunned the bike's cylinders and jumped onto the sidewalk, Ava panicked and began to run. As she ran, she could feel the motorcycle gaining ground.

Suddenly, it was next to her. Before she could react, the driver reached out a leather-gloved hand and shoved her. As she fell sideways, her left leg made an odd cracking noise. Paralyzed by pain, she lay on the ground, helpless. Unable to move, she watched the motorcycle turn and bear down on her again. This time, it stopped inches from her prone body. Hovering over her, the motorcyclist lifted his visor and stared down at her, cold-eyed.

Ava immediately recognized the man. It was her tall dark-haired stranger.

The man looked at her, smiling oddly. "Death comes when you least expect it," he said. He pulled a gun out of his leather jacket and aimed it straight at her head.

"I know who you are," Ava announced in a flash of intuition. Still smiling, the man pulled the trigger. Everything went black.

With a start, Ava woke. Flailing her arms, she got caught in the bed covers. She sat up, happy to discover that she was in her own bed alive and not dead on the quay with a bullet hole in her forehead.

Just to be sure that it was really all a dream, she moved her left leg under the covers and wiggled her toes. They were fine. She moved her right leg and wiggled her right toes. They were fine, too.

With a relieved sigh, she threw her legs over the side of the bed. Her apartment was on the top floor of an 18th century building on the rue des Saints-Pères in the 6th arrondissement of Paris, just up the street from the Seine River and her book stand.

The large open space had been cobbled together from a series of small rooms that were originally used for maids. The apartment had white walls, exposed beams, and a glass roof that made the apartment bright on even the darkest of days.

Curiously, there was a stairway in the far corner that led to a small round room in a tower.

Looking up at the light pouring in from overhead, she estimated that it was 6:45. She checking the clock on the bedside table. It read 6:55.

She smiled.

This was proof that she was becoming a Parisian. Her inner clock was synchronizing with her environment.

Hopping out of bed, she slipped her feet into flip-flops and made her way to the kitchen. The wooden floors creaked as she walked across the large room to the tiny kitchen in the corner of the apartment.

Halfway there, she stopped to choose a record from her late uncle's collection. Deep in concentration, she hesitated between *Beggars Banquet* by the Rolling Stones and *Strange Days* by the Doors. *Beggars Banquet* won.

She removed the record from the shelf and eyed the dedication on its cover:

To Charlie. It was a great tour.

The band members' signatures were under the dedication.

As "Sympathy for the Devil" began to fill the apartment, Ava smiled, amused. The idea that the late Charles Sext, a former Scotland Yard Inspector, had once been known as Charlie and had worked as a roadie for the Rolling Stones was hard to believe.

But then Charles Sext had a past.

Unless Ava got started, she wouldn't have a past -- good or bad.

Maybe the tall dark-haired stranger was just what she needed to jump start an interesting life. If Charles Sext, ex-roadie, could become a Scotland Yard Inspector and then a Paris bookseller/sleuth, she, a former employee of one of London's top PR agencies, could undergo a similar transformation.

More determined than ever to discover why someone had tried to kill the dark-haired man yesterday, she filled the tea kettle with water and put it on. As she measured out green tea and poured it into the teapot, she thought back to what she had said to the man in her dream…

I know who you are.

If she'd said it, it must be true.

Before she could force this information from her sub-conscious, something rubbed up against her bare legs. She jumped, startled.

"What the?"

Looking down, she sighed. A medium-sized black cat was staring up at her with slanted, green eyes as it meowed impatiently.

"Mercury? What are you doing here so early?"

Without responding, the cat turned and walked to a

bowl in the corner. His bowl.

Ava didn't know what the cat's name was. He didn't have any tags on him. She called him Mercury. Like the planet, he appeared most mornings. Mercury was well fed and well groomed. His coat was shiny. For some reason, the cat had decided that it was her job to give him breakfast. For all she knew, her place just might be one stop on his breakfast tour.

As she poured the boiling water into the teapot, she remembered the day Mercury had appeared in her life.

Ava had only been in Paris a week and was feeling lonely. Suddenly, there had been a noise overhead. She had looked up to see a cat squeezing through the skylight that she had cracked open for air. The cat had jumped down and marched over to a cabinet in the kitchen. It stood there, staring at the it, meowing loudly. When she opened the cabinet, she found cat food and a bowl.

Ever since, Mercury had been popping in for breakfast.

"I'm not your slave," Ava grumbled as she went to the cupboard and took out cat food.

As he ate, she sat down at the table and poured herself a cup of tea.

"Who do you think the tall dark-haired stranger is, Mercury?"

The cat ignored her and continued eating. Ava knew that as soon as he finished he would disappear over the rooftops.

Mercury wasn't an affectionate cat who wanted to be petted. That was just fine with Ava. She was not a dyed-in-the-wool animal lover. But then Mercury was not a dyed-in-the-wool people lover.

"In a way, we're perfect for each other," she said to the cat. He ignored her.

Sipping her tea, she ran over the facts.

The only thing she was sure of was that, despite Henri's doubts, someone had tried to kill the man, and that the man was a familiar stranger.

She had seen his face somewhere.

She hadn't lived in Paris long enough to have a lot of familiar strangers in her life.

Where could she possibly have seen him?

Suddenly, Mercury meowed loudly, walked across the room and leapt up on the bookshelves under the window. He knocked over a stack of papers and vanished across the rooftops.

Annoyed, Ava went to pick the papers up.

Leaning over, she saw they were crossword puzzles from the local newspaper. Gerard had saved them for her so she could improve her French.

Every Parisian café had a copy of the local paper on its bar. While having coffee, people would page through it to check sporting results, their horoscopes or glance at lurid headlines about crime and politics.

Ava froze.

Of course!

She must have seen the man in the newspaper at Café Zola.

Her heart beating wildly, she walked back to the wooden dining table, opened her laptop and typed in the name of the paper.

If she had seen the man in it, her task wouldn't be too difficult. Ava never glanced at more than the front page.

It took her only twenty minutes to find the man's picture and the story of his disappearance:

Yves Dubois, 61, professor of medieval literature at the Sorbonne University is missing and believed dead. Dubois was in Italy to speak at a seminar when he disappeared during an evening hike on a seaside path known for being dangerous. The Italian Coast Guard called off the search for Dubois when no body was found.

"The area has hundreds of underwater caves and strong undertows. We might never find his body," a Coast Guard spokesperson said.

Ava checked the date on the article. It was dated three weeks earlier.

To discover if Yves Dubois had been found, she typed in "Yves Dubois disappearance".

All the results said the same thing: Yves Dubois was still missing. One article mentioned that he suffered from bouts of amnesia.

She studied the photo in the paper and said the man's name out loud.

Suddenly, she remembered one of her Uncle Charles's rules for sleuthing.

To test a hypothesis, turn it upside down.

A ripple of excitement ran through her as she applied this to the man's appearance at her stand yesterday.

At one point, she had thought he was lingering to steal something. If she applied her late uncle's rule and turned this upside down, it meant that the man had left something.

The notion that a clue was hidden in one of her boxes was exciting. It might even be the name of the man's would-be murderer!

She dashed across the apartment to get dressed. Pulling her long hair back in a ponytail, she slipped on her favorite black jeans, a well-cut T-shirt, a brightly colored flowered jacket (a relic of her London wardrobe) and flat sandals. After splashing water on her face, brushing her teeth, and slapping bright red lipstick on her lips, she left the apartment and rushed down the stairs.

She was a woman on a mission.

She had a mystery to solve.

She might even be on the verge of discovering who had tried to kill Yves Dubois yesterday and why.

As she stepped out into the rue des Saints-Pères, she breathed in deeply, overcome with a sense of well-being.

Her Uncle Charles had been right.

Coming to Paris and becoming a bookseller was just what she needed to change her life. And when you threw in a near murder, it put the whole process on steroids.

CHAPTER 5

Ava was so excited that she ran down the street. Her heart was beating so loudly that she thought it would jump out of her chest. The eerie silence on the streets made it seem even louder. Traffic was almost non-existent as tomorrow was Friday and a holiday. The month of May was special in France. Most years, May was one long month of holidays strung together.

There was International Worker's Day, WWII Victory Day and Ascension Thursday. By taking off one day of work for a holiday that fell on a Friday or a Monday, you could have a 4-day weekend.

But what if the holiday fell on a Tuesday or a Thursday?

You could take two days off and have a 5-day holiday.

And if you threw in the occasional Wednesday and strung those long weekends together, you had a month where nothing much got done in France -- all the more reason to take time off.

What's the point of working when there was no one to work with?

As tomorrow was Friday and a holiday, Paris had already emptied out.

Despite her excitement and the lack of traffic, Ava waited for the red light to turn green before crossing the street. Her death in her dream last night had seemed all too real. There was no use tempting fate.

When she reached her stand, Ava took her keys out and unlocked the padlocks on her green boxes, one by one. For some reason, it was taking longer than usual. When she had unlocked the last box, she threw their tops open and pulled her folding chair off the books.

She glanced right and left. She was alone on the quay. None of the other booksellers were there yet.

She searched through the books, one by one. First, she looked between the book's front and back covers. Then, she paged through the book carefully. After twenty minutes of searching and finding nothing, she changed her system. She now held each book up by its binding and shook it to see if anything fell out. So far, she had found a parking ticket from 2012, a grocery list, a mayonnaise label, a few store receipts and some handwritten notes. Most were without interest, such as a note about a train to Brussels at 11:35.

The note "Tell George no!!!" intrigued her for an instant: *Who was George and "no" to what?*

After hesitating, she discarded it and continued hunting through her books. Thirty minutes later, she had gone through all of them and had found nothing that looked like a clue to the mystery.

Frustrated, she rustled through the knickknacks in search of a note.

She found nothing.

Zero.

Zip.

Nada.

Her search was a failure.

Ava eyed her green boxes, sure she was missing something.

Her eyes ran over her stand from top to bottom. The second time, they stopped on the locks.

She should have seen it immediately.

The locks were on backwards.

That's why it had taken her longer than usual to open them.

Normally, she opened them by turning the key to the

right. This morning, she had had to turn the key to the left.

There was only one person who would have done that: a left-handed bookseller named Henri DeAth.

Ava shoved her lawn chair back in her stand, locked her boxes and crossed the Quai Malaquais.

Her destination -- Café Zola.

Café Zola was almost empty. A regular customer was standing at the counter reading the morning paper, drinking an espresso. Despite the sign outside advertising a continental breakfast of croissants, butter, jam, orange juice and coffee with milk, a regular would rather die than order something like that.

The neighborhood bar was for a quick "*petit noir*", a French espresso.

Or perhaps a croissant.... without the butter and jam.

Behind the bar, Gerard looked up when he saw her enter. "Morning, Ava," he said, smiling.

She froze in her tracks and stared at the cheerful and suddenly loquacious Gerard.

She was right.

Something was up.

Henri was seated on a stool at the far end of the bar. He, too, was reading the morning paper. He beamed innocently when he saw her. "You're an Aquarius, aren't you?" he asked.

Without waiting for a response, he read Ava her horoscope. "Chance encounters will set you on your path."

Ava shook her head. "No, thank you. After my tall dark-haired stranger, I've had enough of horoscopes."

Gerard put a double espresso in front of Ava without her asking. Sipping it, she watched Henri who continued to read. When he closed the paper, she made her move.

"Time to talk?"

Henri nodded and pointed to "his" table in the back. "Time to talk," he said with an assertive nod.

Ava carried her espresso to the table. Henri finished his and followed her. He brought the newspaper and a magazine with him. Ava slid into the red leather bench against the wall. Henri settled into a chair across from her.

"Paris is a different place when it empties out," Henri said casually.

Ava didn't answer. She wondered which of them would crack first.

Henri pointed at the newspaper. "Nothing about a suspicious death in Paris yesterday. Also, I listened to the radio this morning. There was no mention of a fatal car accident. Your tall dark-haired stranger must still be alive."

"Yves Dubois," Ava said.

"Yves Dubois," Henri acknowledged without the faintest surprise.

He knows, Ava thought, wondering how he had learned the man's identity. She waited for Henri to say more. When he began to read the newspaper again, she cracked. "Where is it?"

Henri looked up. "Where is what?"

Ava leaned across the table. "Henri... I may not be a distinguished member of the notarial profession, privy to the deepest and darkest secrets of the French, but I am a Sext, and we have sleuthing in our blood."

Henri laughed out loud. "Your uncle would be proud of you." He handed her a sealed envelope. It was addressed to Mr. Sext and Mr. DeAth.

Ava took the envelope and turned it over in her hands. If this were a Victorian novel, the letter would be sealed with red wax. Instead, it was glued shut.

Gerard appeared out of nowhere with two more espressos. He looked amused by what was going on. Clearly, Henri had filled him in. Ava waited until Gerard left before speaking.

"You didn't read it?" she asked, waving the still-sealed envelope.

"It was left in your stand. I couldn't open it without you."

Astonishing herself, Ava grabbed his hand. "I love you, Henri."

"You were right about the familiar face," Henri said. He handed her a glossy magazine and opened it to a page that recapped the same elements that she had read earlier online. The glossy magazine spread added a detail that the paper hadn't mentioned: Yves Dubois had been in Italy to speak at a seminar on spirituality.

Dumb-founded, Ava put the magazine down. "How did you know who to look for? You didn't see Yves."

Henri handed her a rough sketch of Yves that captured him perfectly.

"Ali?" Ava asked, annoyed that she hadn't thought to ask him if he had seen the man.

"To answer your question, Ali didn't see the accident or the motorcycle. But he saw the man walk up to your stand. I also learned that this wasn't the first time Yves has gone missing."

"The paper I read mentioned amnesia."

"Amnesia seems very convenient as an excuse," Henri said in a voice laced with skepticism.

Ava sipped her coffee. She could see that Henri was waiting for her to open the letter. Despite her desire to learn its contents, she dragged out the inevitable for as long as she could.

After all, two could play this game.

One minute later, Ava opened the envelope. She

removed a sheet of paper and read what was written on it out loud:

Dear Sirs,

I would like to meet with you at 11:30 on Friday, May 7, to discuss the sale of my book collection.

Sincerely,

Yves Dubois.

Ava put the letter down. "But that's today!"

"At 11:30," Henri said.

"What are we going to do?"

"As you don't look like Mr. Sext or Mr. DeAth, I will go there at 11:30," Henri replied.

"But the letter was in my box!" Ava protested. She checked Yves's address that was written on the bottom of the letter. It was near the Luxembourg Gardens. "You can't go alone! It might be dangerous..."

Henri shook his head. "If Yves Dubois is luring me into a trap, someone has to go to the police. You're the only one who witnessed yesterday's incident."

Ava wanted to protest. However, what Henri was saying made perfect sense. Plus, if Yves Dubois had wanted to confide in her or ask her to appraise his books, he had plenty of time to do so yesterday. Scowling, she took another sip of the strong black espresso. A thought occurred to her. "How did you know to search through the books?"

"I applied one of your uncle's rules: "To test a hypothesis"..."

"…Turn it upside down," Ava said, finishing his phrase.

"I learned a lot from your uncle," Henri said, with tender sadness in his voice.

"Where was the letter?" Ava asked, curious.

"Unfortunately, its location followed a more universal rule: Whenever you look for something, it's always in the first place you look or the last."

"First?" Ava asked.

"Last," Henri admitted with a sigh.

"And the backward locks?"

"A test," Henri confessed. "You passed with flying colors."

Henri's compliment cheered her up. "Do you think Yves will be there?"

Henri shrugged. "I'll only know that when I get there."

"What if it's a trap?" Ava asked, frowning.

"If you haven't heard from me by two o'clock, you should worry."

"That's fine," Ava said.

Surprised, Henri looked up. "Fine? What does that mean?"

"While you're doing that, I'll be waiting for the chance encounter that will set me on my path," Ava replied.

Astonished, Henri looked at her, worried.

CHAPTER 6

Sitting in the shade of a tall tree on the Quai Malaquais, Ava
watched people stroll by.

Never had a morning gone by so slowly.

She almost wished for the appearance of another tall
dark-haired stranger in danger to make time go faster.

Twisting in her chair, she thought back to the letter that
Henri had discovered that morning. In one hour, Henri
would go to Yves Dubois's apartment near the Luxembourg
Gardens.

Would Yves Dubois be there?

Was it a trap?

Ava had no idea. She would only know when Henri told
her afterwards. There was something fundamentally unfair
about that. After all, Yves Dubois was her dead man! She

sighed heavily. No one had ever said that life was fair.

Unable to still her racing mind, she stood up and strode over to the wall that gave onto the quay and the Seine River below. Watching the *Bateaux Mouches* navigate down the river only riled her up more. Every boat on the river appeared to be moving in slow motion, if moving at all.

"I'll take these," a voice said from nowhere.

Startled, Ava turned. A lanky young man wearing a backpack was holding up two vintage postcards. The man handed her a five-euro note. As she gave him his change, she tilted her head to read the time on his watch.

"It's 10:40," the man said, holding it up for her to see.

'Thanks," Ava said, embarrassed.

When she found herself minutes later peering over a woman's shoulder to check the time, Ava decided that action was needed. At this rate, she'd be a nervous wreck before noon. Leaning against the wall, she took out her invisible notebook. Her invisible notebook was where she noted down things she wanted to remember.

If she was going to solve this case with Henri, she needed to be organized. She decided to set up rules.

Holding her imaginary pen in the air, Ava concentrated and then began to write.

Rule #1… *Keep your eye on any tall dark-haired strangers who appear in your life.*

If she had kept her eye on Yves yesterday, she would have certainly learned more. She gnawed on the end of her imaginary pen and continued.

Rule #2... *It's never what you suspect.*

Now while Rule #2 might appear to be a reformulation of her late Uncle Charles's rule on reversing hypotheses, Ava felt this rule was necessary to keep her overly active imagination in check.

At that moment, a large tourist bus lumbered to a halt next to the statue of the woman with a sword. It opened its doors to let its passengers off. As she watched the tourists spill out, she half-expected Yves Dubois to be among them. With a sigh, she realized that unless Yves had become a Japanese teenager overnight, she was out of luck

When the group trooped off toward the Pont des Arts, the Arts Bridge, to cross over to the Louvre, Ava wondered why she hadn't seen Yves slip the envelope in a book. She had been so sure that he was going to steal something that she had watched him like a hawk. Yet, she still hadn't seen him do it.

Ava added another rule.

Rule #3... *Pay attention to what's going on around you.*

"How much is this?" a male voice asked.

Startled, Ava jumped. A bald-headed man with a small white dog was standing next to her, holding a 1980 Paris guidebook.

Ava took the book and opened is back cover. The price sticker was missing. She glanced at the man.

Had he removed it hoping she wouldn't remember the price?

After all, someone who bought a forty-year-old guidebook was odd.

Remembering Rule #2, Ava looked in the front of the book. The price sticker was there.

"It's twenty euros," Ava said.

The man paid her and walked off.

That was a classic example of Rule #2 in action: *It's never what you suspect. Look at the facts.*

The man hadn't removed the price sticker: she had put it in the wrong place.

Unable to resist, she checked the time on her cell phone. It was now eleven. In thirty minutes Henri would meet with Yves Dubois. Ava felt like she was going to explode.

"Did you read your horoscope today?" Ali asked.

Ava whirled around and stared at him. He was standing next to her. "Why is everyone creeping up on me today? I didn't see you arrive."

"I just got here," Ali said. "Henri told me to be here by eleven to watch your stand."

Ava's face lit up like a Christmas tree. "Watch my stand?"

"Aren't you the lookout woman on this caper?"

"When did you speak with Henri?"

Ali shrugged. "I don't know exactly. Maybe an hour ago."

Henri did want her to be there!

Ava was so overjoyed that she had to keep herself from jumping in the air.

Ali straightened her postcards. "By the way, the motorcycle was meant to scare the man not kill him."

"You didn't see it. How do you know that?"

Ali pointed at the sidewalk that ran down the quay. "The sidewalk is narrow and was packed with people. It took skill not to hit the man or anyone else."

Ava studied the sidewalk. Ali was right.

"Why would someone want to scare him?" she asked.

"That's what you and Henri have to discover."

"Ali, I promise you that I will watch your stand on the snowiest day of the year to thank you for this."

"As it almost never snows in Paris that's a safe bet." Ali took a package wrapped in old newspaper out of the messenger bag hanging over his shoulder. He handed it to her.

"What's this?" she asked.

"One of Hassan's new flea market finds."

Ava unwrapped the newspaper wrapping.

Two pale yellow porcelain rabbits stared up at her.

It was another set of salt and pepper shakers, just like the one she had sold the day before. Yellow would go perfectly in her kitchen. It was too bad she had to sell them. She rewrapped them and walked toward her stand like someone heading to the guillotine.

"Ava, a word of advice," Ali said with a smile.

She turned.

"If you don't put the rabbits in your stand, they don't fall under the "*if it's in the stand, it has to be sold*" rule."

Grinning, Ava handed the package back to him. "Thanks, I'll pick them up later."

Suddenly wary, she eyed the package, remembering rule #3: *Pay attention to what's going on around you.* The newspaper certainly fell into that category.

Seeing the expression on her face, Ali shook his head and laughed. "I checked. No horoscope. It's the horse racing results. Unless you plan on betting on a race, in which case they recommend "Lightning" in the fourth, you're safe."

Traffic was light as Ava pedaled her *Velib'* bike, Paris's version of a bike share, up the Quai Malaquais. She turned onto the narrow rue Bonaparte, a street lined with art galleries and continued through the Saint-Germain-des-Prés district with its chic clothing stores and trendy cafés. She parked her bike in the St. Sulpice bike station near the enormous St.

Sulpice Church and its fountain with the grimacing stone lions she so liked. She walked the remaining two blocks to the Luxembourg Gardens.

When she arrived, she checked her phone. It was now 11:18.

She had twelve minutes before Henri would arrive.

While being fifteen to twenty minutes late was perfectly acceptable in France, Henri had been a notary. This meant he was always on time and did things when they needed to be done. Henri would be arriving exactly at 11:30, not a minute earlier or a minute later.

Ava quickly identified the building that corresponded to the address on Yves Dubois's letter. It was situated catty-corner across from the Luxembourg Gardens on the rue de Vaugirard.

She stood on the corner and eyed the surrounding area.

First order of business: *Where should she stand?*

Had she known about this earlier, she would have had time to consider the pros and cons of the various possibilities. Now, she only had a few minutes to decide.

She tried standing at the intersection. When the light turned green and Ava didn't cross, the woman next to her also remained on the sidewalk, peering right and left as if Ava had some special knowledge that a speeding vehicle would appear and knock them both down. Annoyed, Ava crossed the street.

She entered the gardens through the high iron gates next to the Luxembourg Museum. Striding past a gigantic bronze statue, she waded through the grass to the bushes that ran along the high iron fence. As she walked, the grass tickled her ankles.

Glancing around to be sure that no park guards were nearby, she crept through the bushes to the fence and peered through it. A tall streetlight was directly in front of her. This was a perfect spot to hide. She had a clear view of Yves's building, and the bushes and streetlight camouflaged her presence.

She checked the time.

It was 11:23.

In seven minutes, Henri would be there.

Standing in the bushes, Ava, who had become an avid student of Parisian history since moving to the city, ran over what she knew about the gardens.

Queen Marie de Medici, who was noted for her political intrigues, extravagant spending and patronage of the arts, created the gardens in 1612. They covered 25 hectares and ran between the Latin Quarter and Saint-Germain-des-Prés. Divided into French gardens and English gardens, the Luxembourg Gardens were one of Ava's favorite spots for an early evening walk when she felt homesick. All she had to do was head to the English gardens, and she immediately felt better.

Antsy, she crept forward and eyed the front of Yves's building. It was 11:28. Henri's arrival was imminent.

At exactly 11:30, a taxi pulled up and Henri stepped out.

He was dressed in dark blue trousers, a crisp white shirt and an elegantly cut jacket that looked Italian, a far cry from his usual uniform of jeans and a dark blue shirt. Ava thought he looked very smart.

He strode up to the building's double coach doors, pressed on the entrance button and disappeared inside.

Ava stood there, waiting. Shifting nervously, she wondered what she was waiting for. Unless Henri fell out of a window onto the street below, there was nothing more she could do until he left the building.

After a few minutes, her phone rang. She fumbled through her pockets for it.

Why, oh why, does everything happen at once? Ava wondered as she pulled her phone out. Just as she was going to turn it off, she saw that the call was from Henri. She answered instantly. "Henri?" she whispered, breathless.

Instead of Henri's voice, she heard a woman speaking: "Yves sent you this?" the melodious woman's voice asked.

Ava stared down at her phone, puzzled.

It took her an instant to realize that Henri had called her

so she could listen in. Looking up, Ava could see Henri standing in an open window on the third floor. A chic blond woman in her fifties was next to him. A round-faced man with thick wavy hair walked over and joined them.

"Luc, I'm glad you're here. Yves asked Mr. DeAth to come today to appraise his books."

"I told you Yves wasn't dead. He's playing his usual game of cat and mouse," Luc said, triumphant.

"Luc. Not now. Please," Bea said, exasperated. "Where are my manners? Luc Gault, this is Henri DeAth. Luc is my friend and lawyer."

Leaning forward to get a better view of everyone, Ava saw Henri staring straight down at her. She stepped backwards as if burnt. If Henri could see her, Luc or Bea might also notice her. Reluctantly, Ava climbed out of the bushes and walked to a nearby bench with her phone glued to her ear.

For a few moments, she couldn't hear anything. After a long silence, she heard Luc speak.

"He does this because you let him get away with it," Luc said.

"The letter doesn't prove Yves is alive. He could have sent the letter anytime. When did you receive it, Mr. DeAth?" Bea protested.

"Yesterday. I didn't keep the envelope though," Henri

said with regret in his voice.

"You didn't know Yves was missing?" Bea asked.

"Bea. Not everyone knows who the great Yves Dubois is," Luc responded in a voice dripping with sarcasm.

"If this isn't a good time, I can come back," Henri said in a voice so low that Ava could barely hear him.

"No," Luc said. "If Yves sent you the letter, it's because he wanted or needed the books appraised.

Silence.

"What do you think, Bea?" Luc asked.

"For some reason I know nothing of, my husband wanted you to come and see his books. I will honor his wishes. Most of his books are at the abbey," Bea said. "We'll have to go there."

"The abbey is an old ruin Yves inherited outside of Paris," Luc explained.

"My husband inherited it from his late uncle two years ago. It is a ruin," Bea said. "And a money pit."

"I met his uncle once," Luc said. "He was an odd bird. He spent his days holed up in the abbey, studying old manuscripts and books. Yves often joked that his uncle had spent his whole life looking for how many angels could dance on the head of a pin."

"Yves's area of expertise is medieval manuscripts. His uncle was also an expert on the same subject. In fact, Yves's entire family lives and breathes for old parchment. I wonder why he even married me as I couldn't care less about any of that," Bea said in a voice that trailed off. "We could go to the abbey tomorrow."

"I'll drive you there," Luc proposed.

"I was hoping you'd offer," Bea said. "We could leave Paris late afternoon. Would 4 P.M. be good for you, Mr. DeAth? We'll spend the night there. That will give you all of Saturday to look at the books. The abbey itself is very grim, but the setting is lovely. It's in a large forest south of Paris."

"I accept with pleasure. Will your husband be there?" Henri asked.

"Only Yves knows where he'll be. As you've probably understood, as his wife I'm the last one to know."

Suddenly, the voices stopped.

Ava looked at her phone. Henri had cut the call off.

Ava stood up and dashed back into the bushes. She peered out through the fence. The window was empty.

Anxious to speak with Henri, Ava hurried out of the gardens. She slowed at the streetlight. She stood there waiting for Henri to exit.

As the minutes ticked by, she wondered what was taking him so long.

When the building's large coach doors swung open, Ava stepped forward and waved. Instead of Henri, a lanky man in his late twenties carrying a bike over his shoulder came out. He jumped on the bike and pedaled directly toward Ava. Horrified, she froze.

Straddling his bike, the man stopped next to her. He took a flyer out of the messenger bag on his shoulder and taped it to the streetlight.

Hoping that he hadn't seen her wave, Ava stood there, pretending not to notice him.

"This might interest you," the young man said, handing her a flyer.

Ava took it as casually as possible.

"It's tonight. See you there!" The man wheeled his bike around and pedaled off.

Stuffing the flyer into her pocket, Ava looked up. Henri was climbing into a taxi.

She opened her mouth to shout and stopped.

Henri was right.

It was too risky for them to speak near Yves's apartment. As the taxi sped away, she hurried across the street and headed to the *Velib'* station. As she walked, her mind ran over what she had learned:

One: No one knew where Yves was not even his wife.

Two: Yves might be at the abbey or he might not be.

Three: Henri would only learn that tomorrow.

Suddenly, something struck Ava. *Even if Yves were to*

appear at the abbey, she wouldn't know, as she hadn't been invited.

Annoyed, she thrust her hand into her pocket. Her fingers brushed against the flyer. She removed it, unfolded it and began reading.

With each word, her heart began to beat faster. By the time she finished reading it, she was on the verge of a heart attack.

The flyer read:

You didn't find this by accident.

You are a special person.

You have been chosen by the universe.

It is all written.

There will not be a second chance. Seize the opportunity and join us to become a master of the universe.

At the bottom of the flyer, there was a picture of a man.

That man was Yves Dubois!

Her hands shaking, Ava checked the date.

The lecture was taking place that evening at 8 P.M.

She thought of her horoscope… *Chance encounters will set you on your path.*

Maybe the young man was a coincidence and had nothing to do with her horoscope. Or maybe, just maybe, he was the chance encounter that would set her on the path of discovering who was trying to kill Yves.

CHAPTER 7

Ava dashed across the street to her stand on the Quai Malaquais, her fingers clutching the flyer in her pocket as if it were a magical screed. When she reached her stand, she caught her breath, pulled it out of her pocket and read it again, just as she had done at least ten times since leaving the Luxembourg Gardens.

This was a red-letter day in her life.

The universe had chosen her.

She was special.

And most importantly, Yves Dubois was somehow linked to this cosmic relationship.

"How was sleuthing?" Ali asked as he walked over to her, sketchbook in hand.

Sleuthing? Ava was so wrapped up in her flyer that she had completely forgotten Henri and his appointment.

"Great," Ava mumbled, stuffing the flyer in her pocket.

Ali frowned. "Are you OK?"

"Fine. Couldn't be better," she replied a little too quickly.

"Are you sure?" Ali insisted, studying her as if she were a member of an alien species.

"Absolutely."

Ali shifted his weight. He kept his eyes on her. "You sold ten books while you were gone."

"If I were gone more often, profits would soar," Ava joked.

"Are you going to tell me what happened or not?" Ali asked impatiently.

"You mean at Henri's appointment?" Ava asked.

"What else could I mean?"

Ava ignored his remark. "Henri met with Yves's wife, Bea, and her lawyer, Luc. Neither one knew that Yves was alive. But neither seemed surprised to learn that he was. They confirmed that Yves has disappeared before. Henri is going with them to an abbey out in the country tomorrow to appraise books."

Ali swirled his head sideways, looking for Henri. "Where is he?"

"I have no idea. He jumped into a taxi before I could speak with him."

Ali was completely baffled. "Weren't you with him when

he spoke with Bea and Luc?"

"Me? I was hiding in the bushes in the Luxembourg Gardens."

"If you weren't in the apartment, and you haven't spoke with Henri since, how do you know what happened?"

"You've heard the expression "*the walls have ears*"? Well, sometimes they do," Ava replied mysteriously.

Suspicious of Ava's perky mood, Ali studied her. "That's all that happened?"

"That's all," Ava responded as nonchalantly as possible. She strolled over to her lawn chair, sat down, picked up her book and pretended to read.

After one last glance at her, Ali meandered over to his stand. Ava knew that she hadn't fooled him. However, if she had told him what she intended to do, he would try and stop her.

Three hours later, Ava was more and more annoyed with Henri. He had sent her a text message earlier saying that he would be there later. But it was later, and he still hadn't appeared, called or texted.

Fortunately, Ali had entrusted his stand to Ava while he went to the Louvre to sketch. Looking after two stands kept her mind off the lecture this evening. She was actually glad when customers tried to negotiate prices down as it kept her mind occupied. Normally, she hated it when people tried to bargain. Today, she happily played the game. As she negotiated with her customers, she examined each one carefully.

Did they have a secret? Was there something they were hiding?

For the first time, she understood why her Uncle Charles said being a bookseller was like being a detective.... You were able to observe people up close.

At 4:30 P.M., Henri texted her to say he wouldn't be back to the stand this afternoon and suggested coffee the next day. Ava texted him back accepting. Notably, her text message made no mention of her having been chosen by the universe or of her intention to go to the lecture this evening. However, Henri's text message hadn't told her what he had learned since he had left Bea's apartment.

But then Henri was someone who kept his cards close to his chest. If he hadn't told her what he had learned, it was because he still needed information on the case.

The case... Ava almost laughed out loud at the irony of the situation.

Yesterday morning, she had been a bookseller whose greatest happiness was to come to her stand every day. But now that she had tasted the thrill of the chase, so to speak, she realized that she loved sleuthing just as much.

At 6:45, Ava folded up her chair and put a bookmark in her book. In all, she had read two pages and would probably read them again tomorrow as she had no memory of what she had read. She closed Ali's stand and hers. Clutching the package with the pale yellow porcelain rabbits in her hand, she headed back to her apartment to change.

When she reached her apartment, she wondered what a "chosen one" would wear. The young man had been dressed casually. After trying on and eliminating several clothing choices, she decided to wear exactly what she had worn all day. However, she swapped her sandals for sports shoes.

If she had to run after a suspect, she needed to be ready.

At 7:30, she left her apartment, walked down the stairs and headed out onto the street. She was content with herself. It was only day two in her sleuthing career, and she was already hot on the trail of the would-be killer.

She sensed that this was just the beginning.

For a moment, she thought of letting Henri know where she was going in case something happened. She decided against it.

She was a chosen one.

Nothing bad could possibly happen to her.

She would go to the lecture this evening. She would discover what Yves was up to and who was trying to kill him.

Case closed.

After all, she was not only a chosen one… She was also a Sext!

CHAPTER 8

Ava ran her eyes up the facade of the nineteenth century brick and iron industrial building in front of her, searching for some sign of life. There was none. Like the street around her, the building was deserted. Its lights were off, and its doors were locked.

Frowning, she took out the flyer the young man had given her and checked the address.

She was at the right place.

It was the right date.

The iron hands on the clock on the building's wall showed that it was ten minutes to eight. The lecture was supposed to start at eight.

Studying the silent building, she wondered where the others were. For a brief instant, she imagined that there might be no others. Perhaps, she was the sole and unique person the universe had chosen.

Finding that creepy rather than comforting, she strolled over to a bench and sat down. Voices and music wafted up from the Canal St. Martin at the end of the street. The canal was a favorite spot for Parisians on warm evenings.

Sitting on the bench, Ava marveled at how quickly she had arrived. It had taken her only twenty minutes from her apartment to the nearest metro station.

At first, she had considered taking a *Velib'* share bike. But the night was hot and muggy, and she didn't want to arrive drenched in sweat. She had also ruled out taking a bus because of road works. Finally, she had decided to take the metro from the Palais Royal stop to the Gare de l'Est.

Taking the metro from the Palais Royal stop was one of Ava's favorite things to do in Paris. It meant that she got to walk across the Arts Bridge, the pedestrian bridge that she saw every day from her stand.

The bridge was considered the most romantic bridge in Paris. Full moon lovers crowded onto it during the full moon to watch its reflection spread across the water. It was also home to street musicians and painters. People even picnicked on it.

Once she crossed the Arts Bridge to the Seine's right bank, the Louvre Museum was before her in all its majesty. The Louvre and its classical architecture had always fascinated her. After entering the Cour Carrée, a square courtyard that was the site of the original Louvre in the Middle Ages, a quick left led her to the Napoleon Courtyard. There, she would inevitably stop and admire the 20th century glass pyramid designed by I.M. Pei that now served as the museum's main entrance.

Picking up her pace, she would veer right and amble through a dark, high-ceilinged passageway, slowing only to eye massive white marble statues in an interior courtyard. She would exit on the rue de Rivoli, a busy thoroughfare that ran to the Place de la Concorde with its giant Egyptian obelisk.

Dashing across the street, she would continue to the metro entrance in front of the Palais Royal Garden. The entrance was an artwork. Brightly colored glass balls floated in the air over the steps that led to the metro. Every time she walked under the ceiling of glass baubles, Ava felt she was embarking on a magical adventure. Thus, it was fitting that her first trip as a "chosen one" had begun there this evening.

Waiting on the bench, Ava surveyed her surroundings, philosophical.

If, indeed, the universe had chosen her, it would show her a way to the lecture. If not, it was a sign that she hadn't been chosen.

A male voice pulled her from her thoughts.

"You're here for the lecture?"

Ava looked up. A well-built man in his mid-thirties, dressed in a dark T-shirt and khaki cargo shorts with white socks and sandals on his feet, was standing next to her.

"I thought I was in the wrong place," Ava confessed.

"It's hard to find the first time. I don't know why Yves doesn't draw a map."

"Maybe it's a test to see if we really were chosen," Ava joked.

The man laughed. "I never thought of it that way. Follow me."

Ava stood up and followed the man to a door at the far end of the building. The man pressed a buzzer, and the door clicked opened. They walked up the stairs. Their footsteps rang out in the silence. When they reached the third floor, muffled voices began to filter down from above.

"People usually get here early to get a seat," the man said, glancing over his shoulder to speak to her.

When they reached the fourth floor, the man pushed a heavy metal door open.

They were in a small hallway.

A table with a basket on it was across from the door. A donation sign stood next to the basket.

To their left, there was a large room devoid of furniture. Small groups of people were scattered around it. A wooden stage with a microphone was set up in the front of the room.

"You have to take your shoes off," the man said as he slipped his shoes off. He added them to the rows of shoes lined up against the wall.

Ava removed her sports shoes and placed them with the others.

The man whispered to her. "A word of advice. If you have trouble sitting cross-legged, I recommend choosing a spot by the wall. That way, you can lean back."

Leaving her, he strode into the room and threaded his way through the people seated on the floor.

Standing at the entrance in her bare feet, Ava felt a hostile stare directed at her. The stare was coming from a striking-looking woman in her late twenties with curly blond hair and strong features.

Ava ignored the stare and continued to study the room. There were about thirty-five people milling about. Some were sitting. Others were standing. Most were speaking softly to each other. One or two had their eyes closed and appeared to be meditating. Others stared at the stage in nervous anticipation. Neither Yves nor the man who had given her the flyer was in the room.

Ava padded barefooted to the back of the room, searching for a free spot against the wall. Finding one, she slipped down and crossed her legs. She smiled and looked left and right, hoping to strike up a conversation with her neighbors and learn more. However, the people next to her ignored her and continued speaking among themselves in hushed tones.

As the minutes ticked by with no signs of the lecture starting, Ava decided to do some exploring.

Standing up, she made her way back to the entrance. When she had first come in, she had noticed a red velvet curtain on her left. She headed to the curtain. After checking that no one was paying attention to her, she pulled it open and slipped through it. She was in a long hallway. There were several doors on the hallway's left side.

She stood there, eyeing the doors.

It reminded her of a game show: Which door was Yves Dubois hiding behind?

Tiptoeing down the hallway, Ava examined the first door. Loud voices coming from an open door at the end of the hallway attracted her attention.

They were women's voices, and they were arguing.

Ava crept toward the door, thankful that her bare feet made no sound on the tiled floor. Noticing a gilded mirror on the wall opposite the door, Ava stepped back until she could see what was happening in the room reflected in it.

Ava saw two women in the mirror. The first woman was slim. In her early thirties, she had long red hair and porcelain skin. She was sitting on the edge of a table, wearing jeans and an oversized white shirt. The second woman was a solid woman in her fifties with long silvery hair that hung down her back in a braid. A gauzy dress floated around her. There was a certain "earth mother" aspect to her.

It took Ava a few seconds of listening to identify who was who. The redhead's name was Margot. The earth mother was Kris.

Pressing her body against the wall, Ava listened to what they were saying as she watched their actions in the mirror.

"Kris, there aren't even fifty people here. We should have waited for Yves," Margot said as she tapped the table nervously with her fingers.

Kris shook her head. "What if Yves doesn't come back? Does that mean the work stops?"

Margot gasped. "Of course, Yves will come back. If he were dead, the Italian police would have found a body."

"The point I'm trying to make is that the work is more important than any one person," Kris said. "The work has to continue, Yves or no Yves."

"Yves is special. He was chosen," Margot countered.

"We were all chosen," Kris said in a cutting tone. "You and I were chosen before Yves."

Margot's expression showed her disagreement. "Yves has a gift. When he speaks, people believe in the work.

Without him, there would only be five or six of us."

"You don't believe in the power of the work?" Kris asked angrily.

"Of course, I do. You should have talked to Max and me before sending out emails and flyers to hold a lecture tonight," Margot said.

Kris's face went red. "Despite your maneuvering to get close to Yves, you're not in charge. Even if you had succeeded in seducing him, it wouldn't have changed anything. He'd forget you like he forgot the others."

Shocked, Margot jumped off the table. She clenched her fists in anger. "How dare you. Just because he was never interested in you…"

Kris cut her off. "The work is more important than any one person, Yves is just a messenger."

"The work. The work. I'm sick of hearing you talk about the work," Margot said in rebellion.

"Then maybe you shouldn't be one of us," Kris responded with a steely glare.

'That's not for you to decide," Margot said. "When Yves returns, he'll sort this out."

Kris fell silent.

Ava crept forward to see what was happening. As she moved, Kris stepped out into the hallway and stared at her.

"Can I help you?" Kris asked.

"I was looking for the bathroom," Ava responded as innocently as possible.

Kris crossed her arms and eyed Ava suspiciously. "You went right past it. It's two doors down."

"Thank you. It wasn't marked. I didn't know," Ava said.

Before Ava could leave, Kris moved and blocked her path.

Ava caught her breath, sure that Kris was about to accuse her of lying or maybe even attack her.

Instead, Kris smiled warmly at her. Her hostility had vanished. "Excuse my brusque tone. Of course, you couldn't have known where the bathroom was. This is your first time here. Welcome. You are a chosen one."

Margot entered the hallway and eyed Ava, silent.

Thrown off kilter by Kris's odd behavior and Margot's stare, Ava retreated to the bathroom. When she reached it, she opened the door, stepped inside and locked it behind her. Hearing the lock click close, she breathed a sigh of relief. She was safe for the moment.

To calm her nerves, she ran the cold water. She splashed some on her wrists and temples. Its coolness felt divine and helped her calm down. Her encounter with Kris had destabilized her.

As the water continued to run, Ava went over what she had just learned.

One: Neither woman knew where Yves was.

Two: He was a ladies' man, a 'love them and leave them' type of guy.

Three: The "you have been chosen" group existed before Yves.

Four: There was no love lost between Kris and Margot.

Hearing the loud screech of a microphone reverberating from the main hall, Ava turned off the water, dried her hands and stepped out into the now empty hallway. The door at the end of the hall was closed. For a second, she considered creeping down and searching it but decided against it.

She hurried to the main room. As she entered it, Kris's words echoed through her mind...

"Welcome. You are a chosen one."

As she slipped into her spot against the wall, Ava wondered just what the universe had chosen her for.

CHAPTER 9

No one was on the stage in the front of the room. A lone spotlight shone down on it, accenting this emptiness.

Suddenly, the light went off, and the room was plunged in darkness.

People fell silent. Ava pressed her back against the wall and craned her neck to better see what was going on. She caught her breath in anticipation.

Something was about to happen.

She wasn't the only one to sense that. She could feel it all around her. The crowd was filled with a growing sense of excitement.

Suddenly, the stage lit up revealing Kris and Margot. Kris stepped to the microphone and gazed around the dark room with a warm, almost beatific welcoming smile on her face, a smile that beamed goodness and love.

"Welcome. You are here because you were chosen," Kris said, opening her arms wide as if to embrace the crowd.

A ripple of acknowledgement ran through the room.

Ava felt a powerful force emanating from the woman. Anyone who got on Kris's wrong side would not be in for a pleasant experience.

"Tonight, Margot will speak first," Kris said, waving her arm at the woman next to her.

Ill at ease, Margot pushed her long red hair behind her ears and stepped to the microphone.

Ava studied her. Margot certainly didn't have the air of the seductress that Kris had accused her of being. If anything, Margot looked like a schoolgirl forced by the teacher to speak in front of the class.

Biting her lip and squeezing her hands together, Margot gazed out across the dark room. After a long silence, she spoke. Her wavering voice betrayed her nervousness. "The universe has chosen you. Maybe you don't know why. You might even ask yourself: "*Why me, why not another?*" I can't answer that. That's one of the true mysteries of the universe. I do promise you one thing. The secrets you will learn here will awaken the flame in you, and that flame will reveal your path in the work and your rightful place as a master of the universe."

Hearing the words "master of the universe", Ava perked up. Now they were getting somewhere. Shifting her body, she unwound her legs and pulled her knees against her chest. No matter what position she took, it was torture. Being a chosen one wasn't all milk and honey. Glancing around, she saw that everyone was enraptured.

"The secret wisdom of the ages will be revealed to you. This wisdom will change your life. In turn, you will change the world," Margot said. As she spoke these last words, she underwent a subtle transformation. Her entire being now exuded confidence.

Kris appeared and took the microphone from Margot. "Thank you for your inspirational words. It's now time for testimonials. I want each of you to tell us how the work has changed your life."

One after another, people stood and spoke about their experience with the work. Some said it had given meaning to their lives. Others felt empowered by it. One man was so moved that he burst into tears, unable to speak.

Ava didn't believe for a moment that she or anyone else here had been chosen to become a master of the universe. But if it were true, it would indeed be a heady experience.

She closed her eyes and imagined sitting in her green and white lawn chair on the Quai Malaquais as tourists strolled past, unaware that the woman in front of them was a master of the universe. Possessing a secret like that could quickly become intoxicating.

Opening her eyes, Ava saw with horror that Kris was staring straight at her. In fact, unless she was hallucinating, Kris was speaking about her.

"This evening, we have a new person with us... another person chosen by the universe to become part of the work and our lives. No, let me restate that. She has always been part of the work. It was only that the universe chose not to reveal it to her earlier. Would like to stand and introduce yourself?"

Panicked, Ava saw heads turning toward her. There was no getting out of it. Reluctantly, she rose to her feet. Her heart was beating so loud, she was afraid it would drown out her voice.

For an instant, she froze, unable to speak. Then she swallowed, opened her mouth and forced words to come out of it. "I'm Ava. I'm grateful to be here with you. I'm grateful the universe has chosen me."

"When did the revelation come to you?" Margot asked, stepping forward.

Ava shifted her weight as she debated how to respond. She could say that the revelation had happened that very afternoon when a young man on a bike gave her a flyer, but she had a better, more daring idea. "Yves Dubois told me about the work."

Kris reeled back, stunned, while Margot stared. Other eyes looked at Ava, in admiration and jealousy.

"You are fortunate. Having Yves discover your connection to the universe is a rare gift," Kris said.

The mere mention of Yves caused people in the room to whisper. Ava took advantage of this to slide back to the floor.

A waif-like woman raised her hand. "Where is Yves?"

A murmur ran through the crowd.

A bearlike man with a thick beard and long shaggy hair pulled back in a ponytail stood up. "Is he coming back?"

Ava stretched out her left leg that was going numb. She followed what was going on attentively. *Maybe, just maybe, someone would drop a clue as to why someone wanted to kill Yves.*

"Why isn't he here? Why hasn't he sent us his weekly missive?" a tiny Asian woman asked.

Her question seemed to synthesize the doubts in the room. Shouts of "Where is Yves?" rang out.

Kris raised her hands in the air and used them to quell the growing revolt. As Margot eyed her nervously, Kris stepped away from the microphone and spoke directly to the room. "Yves couldn't be here tonight, but he wanted you to come this evening. The work continues with or without him."

A hush fell over the room.

"But he'll be back?" the bearlike man asked with insistence.

A flash of anger moved across Kris's face, only to be replaced instantly by a beatific smile. "What a question. Of course, Yves will be back. I spoke with him just minutes ago."

Margot spun her head and stared at Kris, incredulous.

"What did he say?" a woman asked, breathless.

The room was silent. Everyone else stared at Kris.

"Yves has made an important discovery, something that will advance the work. He'll soon be back to share it with us. Until then, he asks that you continue on your path. His spirit will guide you until his return," Kris said.

A rustle of excitement and relief ran through the crowd. The idea of a new revelation fired up the participants, and they began to whisper excitedly among themselves.

Ava was astonished. When Kris and Margot were speaking earlier, Kris had no idea where Yves was. She didn't even think he was alive.

And now there had been a call...

Could he have called while Ava was in the bathroom? If so, why didn't Margot know about the call?

Kris turned and left the stage. Margot followed her off.

Without fanfare, the lights went on.

The lecture was over.

Ava stayed seated and watched everyone leave. No one looked special. In fact, people looked totally ordinary. Maybe the universe had deliberately disguised the chosen ones as your everyday ordinary Parisians and one transplanted Londoner.

The blond-haired woman who had stared at Ava earlier ran across the room followed by the man who had showed Ava the way in.

"Lili. Wait," the man hissed as he dashed behind her.

Intrigued, Ava stood up and hurried to the entrance. As the man grabbed his sandals and pulled them on, Lili scooped up her shoes and dashed out in tears.

Puzzled, Ava sat down and put her shoes on. She stopped to put five euros in the basket.

Frowning, she saw there was hardly any money in it.

At that moment, the young man who had given her the flyer appeared and began to gather up everything on the table.

Ava smiled at him. The young man looked right through her as if she didn't exist and walked away. Annoyed, Ava headed to the exit. Just then, Margot appeared from behind the curtain. She stared at Ava with an odd expression on her face.

Ava left. She ran down the steps, slowing only when

she reached the street.

Something strange was going on.

She didn't believe that Kris had spoken with Yves. In fact, every part of her screamed that Kris was lying.

If Yves had called, why hadn't Kris told Margot about it?

Margot's baffled expression when she heard about the call spoke for itself.

Also, if Yves had called, the call couldn't have lasted more than two to three minutes, the time Ava was in the bathroom. If someone called after being missing for weeks, you would be relieved to learn they were safe. But the Kris who had walked out on stage didn't appear any different from the Kris who had no idea if Yves was dead or alive minutes earlier.

Puzzled by what she had learned, Ava headed down the street toward the canal. She regretted that she hadn't recorded the lecture on her phone. Henri might be able to glean information from it that she couldn't.

Thinking of Henri, she felt guilty.

She should have called him earlier to tell him where she was going. Instantly, a feeling of righteous indignation ran through her, chasing away any feelings of guilt.

If Henri had taken the time to call her and reveal what he had learned, she would have told him where she was going.

The Canal St. Martin was a four and a half kilometer long canal that ran from the Canal de L'Ourcq in the northeast of Paris to the Seine River. Under Napoleon, the canal had been used to bring fresh water into the city to stamp out cholera. Later, it became a waterway to bring in grains and other foods. Today, it was for pleasure boats and people wanting to spend a nice evening out near the water.

As the weather was beautiful and it was the eve of a long weekend, the banks of the canal were packed. Musicians, jugglers, picnickers, and people of all ages were spread out along its banks. Some people were escaping the heat of their apartments. Others were enjoying sitting along the tree-lined canal.

Ava strolled down its banks, noting what she had learned in her invisible notebook.

First. Yves Dubois was some sort of guru. People were chosen. Although if her manner of being chosen was the standard, she had doubts about the universe's selection process.

Ava slowed.

Maybe, just maybe, she really was a chosen one.

She entertained that idea for a brief instant. According to Rule #2, it's never what you suspect. So as she was sure she hadn't been chosen, there was a slight chance she had been…. Say a .000001% chance.

She held her head higher on the off-chance it was true and continued taking notes.

Secondly. What was a master of the universe? To Ava, it sounded like the name of some expensive video game.

Thirdly. The work had secrets and revelations, one of which Yves had supposedly just discovered. Also, the work existed before Yves.

Lastly. She had learned nothing about Yves's disappearance.

Walking past a gourmet food truck, Ava's stomach growled. Stepping into line, she studied the menu. She was hesitating between vegan chili and a vegetarian burrito when she heard a familiar voice speaking to the food truck worker.

She recognized the voice immediately.

It was the man from the lecture.

Peering over the person in front of her, Ava saw that that the man was with Lili.

Ava ducked when they walked off with their food. She watched them head to the side of the canal. They sat down to eat with their feet dangling over the water's edge.

She thought of dashing right over but decided to order food first. If they did see her, she would look less suspicious that way. Besides, sleuthing had made her hungry.

When it was her turn, Ava addressed the food truck worker, "What's faster? The vegetarian chili or the vegan burrito?"

The man inside the food truck shook his head. "What are they, in some sort of race?" Laughing at his own humor, he continued, "If you're in a rush, get the chili... Or the burrito. They both take the same time.

"Chile," Ava said. "No, burrito."

Glancing over her shoulder to ensure the couple hadn't disappeared, Ava paid and wandered toward them. She browsed through jewelry a woman was selling from a cloth on the ground near the couple. As she looked at the jewelry, she leaned sideways to catch their conversation.

The couple was arguing.

"Why don't you believe me? Why don't you believe Kris?" the man asked.

"Because we both know it's not possible, Arnaud," Lili responded. "What's Kris up to?"

"Kris? Who cares about her?" Arnaud replied angrily. "Why can't you accept that Yves is alive?"

"If Yves were alive, he would have contacted me. That's how I know he's dead," Lili responded with a cold stare at Arnaud.

Taking a bite of her burrito, Ava moved from the jewelry display to join a small crowd watching a fire-eater on the other side of the couple.

Why was Lili so sure that Yves was dead? Ava wondered as she continued to eavesdrop.

Arnaud was exasperated. "There's only one way to prove to you that Yves is alive. We have to go to the abbey tomorrow."

"I plan to," Lili responded calmly.

Arnaud was flabbergasted. "When did you decide to do that?"

"The moment Kris announced she had spoken to Yves. Someone killed him. I intend to find out who it was and why, no matter where the pieces fall," Lili announced in a threatening tone.

"The seminar is only for the inner circle," Arnaud countered. "Kris won't like it if you appear."

"I don't care what Kris thinks."

"If you're going, I'm coming with you," Arnaud said.

"That's not a good idea," Lili said.

"I'm not asking you, Lili. At 5:10 tomorrow afternoon, I'm catching the train at Gare de Lyon, whether you like it or not. I've had enough of Yves and his manipulative behavior. I wouldn't put it past him to have faked his own death."

"Yves never manipulated anyone," Lili responded, furious.

Angry, Arnaud rose to his feet. "I've had enough of Yves. You treat him like he's a God."

Lili stood up. "You're jealous?"

"Just because I see Yves as the charlatan he is doesn't mean I'm jealous," Arnaud countered. He put his hand on her shoulder. "Why don't you believe me when I tell you he's alive?"

She pushed his hand away. "Because we both know that's impossible."

Arnaud reached for her hand. She moved away from him and walked off. Distraught, Arnaud followed her. Ava stepped toward the edge of the canal to see where they were going.

Suddenly, someone shoved her. She lost her balance. For what seemed like an eternity, she hovered over the water before falling into it. The shock of the ice-cold water caused her to gasp. Floundering in the dark canal, she dropped her burrito and sank beneath the water's surface. Panicking, she pulled herself up. She forced herself to tread water.

Two men jumped into the canal to save her. Water splashed everywhere. There were shouts. Someone threw a life preserver into the water. It landed next to her. The men pushed her toward it, nearly drowning her in the process.

Chaos ensued.

The next thing Ava knew, she was on her back on the

side of the canal looking up at the dark sky.

All around her voices were shouting.

"Call the fire department!"

"No, she needs to go to the hospital. The water is full of bacteria."

"It was a suicide attempt."

"Is she still alive?"

Ava panicked. *Was she dead?*

"I know her. I'll see that she gets home," a reassuring male voice said from afar.

Hearing the familiar voice, Ava looked up and saw Henri staring down at her with a troubled expression on his face. She blinked once and then a second time. Each time, Henri was still there.

She wasn't dead.

She wasn't delirious.

She was alive, and Henri had somehow appeared to help her.

When she looked up again, Henri was gone, and the young man with the flyer was staring down at her.

Ava blinked. When she opened her eyes, the young man was gone.

"It's OK. It's OK. The show's over," Henri said as he helped Ava up. "Are you OK, Ava?"

She reached out and touched his arm to be sure he

was real. "I want to go home," she said. Looking at the crowd around her, Ava shivered.

Her first day as a chosen one had not gone well.

CHAPTER 10

Spread out across a field of brightly colored tulips, hundreds of giant blue and yellow porcelain rabbits surrounded Ava as she sat on the ground, dazed. The rabbits towered over her. Their painted-on eyes stared down at her in concern. The eyes seemed to be warning her of something. Overhead, a large white cloud floated by. A woman's voice echoed down from it, murmuring over and over again like a litany, "Ava is the chosen one."

Suddenly, a loud ringing sound startled the rabbits.

One by one, they jumped up and hopped away, leaving Ava alone with the voice and the flowers.

The ringing grew louder.

Groggy, Ava rolled over, opened her eyes and looked around. The field of tulips was gone, and there wasn't a rabbit in sight. She was in bed in her apartment. Her head hurt, and her eyes felt heavy. In fact, her entire body ached.

With a frown, she located the source of the ringing.

It was her Uncle Charles's old-fashioned wind up alarm clock.

Ava reached out and hit the metal button on top of it several times until the ringing stopped. Sitting up, she pulled the clock over to check the time.

It was 9 A.M.

Memories of yesterday evening's spiritual lecture and of her fall into the canal came rushing back to her. She had a vague memory of Henri helping her home.

"Henri!" she shouted out.

The only response was an insistent meowing coming from the far end of the apartment.

A bit woozy, Ava stood up and headed to the kitchen where Mercury was finishing his breakfast. Lifting his head, the cat greeted her with a purr and immediately went back to eating.

Ava strode over to the cat and crouched down in front of him. "You got Henri to give you breakfast? Where's your loyalty? You could have waited until I got up so we could have breakfast together."

In response, Mercury continued eating.

"I understand. Your stomach comes before loyalty," Ava said with a frown as she rose to her feet. She poured herself some cold coffee and headed over to the large wooden table that divided the kitchen from the rest of the apartment.

A pair of pale yellow rabbit salt and pepper shakers was sitting in the middle of the table next to a large vase of flowers. The rabbits' eyes were staring at her. If the rabbits could speak, Ava had no doubt that they would ask her how she ended up in the canal.

Sighing, she sank down into a chair. Sipping her coffee, she noticed a piece of paper propped up against the vase.

It was a note was from Henri:

Ava,

As you're reading this, it means you survived your evening dip in the canal. I gave you a sleeping pill. Don't worry if you're groggy.

Breakfast together at 9:45 to discuss the case?

H.

Instantly, Ava's tiredness vanished.

Henri's last four words had given her wings.

Henri wanted to discuss the case with her!

That meant that Henri DeAth considered that she, Ava Sext, was a fellow sleuth.

Instantly, her mind went into overdrive as she ran over everything that had happened the night before. She tried to draw up a basic outline of the facts to present to Henri. As she thought, a strange smell wafted up to her nose. She took a deep breath in and frowned.

It was a damp brackish odor.

Sniffing her arm, she realized with horror that the odor was coming from her.

Jumping up, Ava made a mad dash to the bathroom, thankful that she had had bought her favorite fig shower gel earlier that week. She slowed only to choose a record from her Uncle Charles's record collection.

Feeling the sun streaming through the glass ceiling overhead, Ava chose the album *It's a Beautiful Day* by the band of the same name. She put the record on the record player and cranked up the volume.

As the first notes echoed through the apartment, she stepped into the shower and let the hot water wash away any traces of the Canal St. Martin. For a brief instant, her mind drifted from the case. She was lost in a world of good music and perfumed shower gel. Reinvigorated, she stepped out of the shower and pulled a fluffy bath towel around her.

In the grand scheme of things, her dip in the canal was nothing compared to the danger Yves Dubois was in: a danger that she and Henri would soon put an end to.

By coming to her stand, Yves had put his life in their hands.

She and Henri would not let him down.

She padded over to her closet and looked at her wardrobe. As this was her first official day as a detective, she needed to dress the part. After hemming and hawing, she decided on a variation of what she had worn the day before -- black jeans and a white T-shirt. This morning, she added a short-sleeved khaki jacket that had lots of pockets.

Once dressed, she headed to the door. She stopped and glanced at her reflection in the large antique mirror in the entryway. She frowned. Her look was missing something.

Hunting through her pockets, she pulled out a tube of bright red lipstick and swiped some on her lips. Rather appropriately, the shade was called "Deadly Red".

She rechecked her appearance. Red lips gave her an air of glamour and mystery. Just what was needed.

Closing the door behind her, she headed down the stairs and out into the street. Café Zola was almost empty when she arrived. The only customer, a regular she knew by sight, was drinking an espresso at the bar. Ava strode past him and headed straight to Gerard who was putting coins in the cash register.

"Is Henri here?" Ava asked.

Gerard looked up and chuckled. "Heard you had a swim last night?"

"It's not funny, Gerard," Ava responded. "I could have drowned."

"I doubt that. You're like your uncle. You're made of sterner stuff," Gerard said. Turning, he picked up a metal egg stand with hard-boiled eggs in it. He set it down in front of her. "Have an egg, you'll feel better."

Despite her feelings being ruffled by his teasing, Ava couldn't resist his offer. The eggs were free-range eggs from a farm near Paris. Gerard could go on for hours about what type of chicken they were from and how they were raised. Ava was sure he would be able to show the chickens' school and athletic records if asked.

Gerard put a small plate in front of her. She reached out and took the egg. It was still warm. With a smile, she peeled off its shell. Shifting the egg from one hand to the other, she sprinkled sea salt on it and bit into it. As the flavor spread to her taste buds, she sighed a contented sigh. "It's divine."

"Next time, try it with salt and cumin. It's even better," Gerard said like a proud father. He added as an aside, "Henri's waiting for you down by the river."

Ava nodded and finished her egg, savoring every bite. Wiping her mouth, she turned to leave. Seeing the morning paper on the counter, she couldn't resist reading her horoscope. Given how accurate her last two horoscopes had been, she decided it was a good idea to check today's horoscope. After all, forewarned was forearmed.

Ava ran her finger down to Aquarius. Her horoscope read:

You will cross distant waters and be tested. Failure will be fatal.

Ava's blood ran cold. *Distant waters?* Could her horoscope be referring to her dip in the Canal St. Martin?

The Canal St. Martin was in Paris. Its waters could hardly be considered distant. In addition, she hadn't crossed them. As she remembered it, she had sunk like a load of lead -- an inglorious moment in her sleuthing career. Somehow, she couldn't imagine her Uncle Charles or Henri getting pushed into a canal.

With a wave to Gerard, Ava left the café, unable to shake the word "fatal" from her mind. Fatal was one of those words you never wanted to hear, along with words like "contagious", "rabid" or "poisonous".

She hurried across the road and strode past her green boxes, sending them a mental hello as she went by. She continued to the Arts Bridge and dashed down the stone steps to its right to reach the lower quay.

Once there, she slowed, struck by the silence.

At street level, even on a holiday like today, you were surrounded by the sound of cars and buses. Next to the river, everything was quieter. The only sounds were those of boats going by or the frantic cry of seagulls circling in the sky overhead. The light on the water was also different. It was brighter and shone like diamonds.

Henri was sitting between two large boats on the edge of

the river. His feet were dangling over the water. The boat to his left was one of Ava's favorite boats on the quay. It was a large schooner made of highly polished wood that had tall masts that soared high in the air. The boat reminded her of a pirate ship. The boat to his right was a low barge whose owner, a friend of Henri's, had turned the deck into a botanical garden. Flowering plants covered the entire deck, perfuming the air around it. Both boats made dull clanking sounds as they rocked up and down in the water.

Henri looked up when Ava strode over.

"Coffee?" he asked, picking up a thermos that was sitting next to a picnic basket.

"Coffee," Ava replied as she sat down, swinging her legs over the edge of the quay. She let her feet dangle over the water. She took the cup Henri handed her and smelled its contents. It was strong and earthy, just what she needed.

As she took her first sip, something occurred to her... She hadn't told Henri about the lecture. How had he learned about it?

"Henri, how did you...?"

He cut her off. "I met a young man coming down the steps in Yves's building. He was carrying a bike over his shoulder as he stuffed flyers into a messenger bag. We bumped into one another, and he dropped some flyers."

"One of which you accidentally managed to keep."

"One of which I deliberately kept," Henri said with a smile.

"Would it be closer to the truth to say that you bumped into him?"

Henri raised his eyebrows, amused. "That's a distinct possibility. You're getting the hang of this rather quickly."

"It must be the same man who gave me the flyer."

"Tall, handsome, strong features... and polite. He excused himself several times when I was the one who had bumped into him."

"Handsome? Maybe..." Ava replied, trying to remember what the young man looked like. She plucked a croissant from the picnic basket next to Henri. "Did you see who pushed me in the water?"

Henri shook his head. "No. There was a crowd around you. You were staring at a couple walking off. I looked at them. The next thing I knew you were in the water."

"Butter," Ava said as she bit into the croissant.

"Butter," Henri confirmed.

In heaven, Ava savored each bite. When she had first come to Paris, eating a croissant had been a special treat. The idea of eating a croissant made with butter seemed incredibly indulgent. And now, eating a croissant with butter had become an everyday occurrence. Somewhere, there had been a slippery slope she had missed. Fortunately, it was too late to go back up it.

Henri poured himself more coffee. "Could your fall have been an accident? There were a lot of people there. Someone might have jostled you in passing."

Ava finished her croissant and took another sip of coffee. "I was listening to the couple. They had been at the lecture. They were arguing about going to a seminar this weekend. When they left, I intended to follow them. Instead, I felt a hand push me in the canal. It was a deliberate shove. Before I knew it, I was in the cold water splashing about," she said, pausing. "Was it a warning? Like for Yves?"

"That's my guess. If someone wanted you to drown, they wouldn't have pushed you in the canal. It's not that deep, and there were loads of people ready to help."

Ava looked Henri directly in the eyes. "Thank you for being there."

Henri poured her more coffee. "That's what partners in crime do. They help each other."

All at once, she remembered something. "Henri, the man with the bike was standing behind you when I opened my eyes."

Henri appeared surprised. "The young man I bumped into? Are you sure?"

"Yes."

"Could he have pushed you?"

"I don't think so. He looked worried. Besides, if he had pushed me, he wouldn't have hung around."

"Perhaps," Henri said. "Was he at the lecture?"

"I only saw him at the end. When he saw me, he didn't recognize me. In fact, he looked right through me like I wasn't even there," Ava said, more vexed than she would like to admit. She might not be a beauty queen, but she liked to think she was memorable.

"He remembered you. You're not someone that's easy to forget," Henri said. "Now tell me what you learned."

Pleased by his comment, Ava ran over everything that had happened. She started with her being chosen, then moved to the conversation between Kris and Margot. She finished with Kris's announcement that Yves had called and would soon be back with an important discovery that would advance the work.

"Did they explain what the work was?" Henri asked.

Ava shook her head. "No. It does eventually lead to becoming a master of the universe."

"A master of the universe?" Henri repeated, incredulous.

"Mostly, the lecture focused on how lucky we were to have been chosen. The people there were zealous true believers. Even I felt different when I left."

Henri sat back. "Are they after people's money?"

"No. No one there looked rich. And there was almost nothing in the donation basket."

Henri poured them both more coffee. He took a croissant for himself and handed one to Ava.

"To recap, before the lecture started, Kris believed that Yves was dead. Yet, before it had ended, she'd spoken with him."

Ava nodded. "Margot, the red-haired woman, was astonished. You could see it in her expression."

Henri frowned. "It's odd that Kris initially believed he was dead, while Margot only thought he was missing. Why didn't Yves tell his inner circle he was alive?"

"Maybe he was afraid," Ava suggested.

"Of the women?"

"Perhaps. Margot also mentioned a man. His name was Matt or Max... something like that. I don't remember. It's possible that Yves did call Kris... But as she was already in the main room when I left the bathroom, I don't see when it could have happened," Ava said.

"And from what you say, Lili is convinced that Yves is dead, and Arnaud knows something about it. The same Arnaud who insists that Yves is alive and is fueling the rumors of his own death," Henri added. He had a thoughtful expression on his face.

"Lili intends to go to the seminar this weekend and discover who killed him."

"Is she one of Yves's conquests?"

Ava nodded. "There's a good possibility of that. Arnaud said she treated Yves like God."

"I'm not surprised that Yves is a ladies' man. I gathered that much from Bea and Luc," Henri said.

After resisting temptation, Ava bit into the second croissant.

It was heaven, pure heaven.

People gave far too much importance to self-control. Sometimes, excess was just what was needed. After a near brush with death, a second croissant was the least Ava could do for herself.

Henri tapped his fingers on the stone quay. "Let's run over the facts. Not what we think we know or what might have happened, but what did happen."

"Yves was alive and well two days ago," Ava said.

"I agree. However, that doesn't mean that he's still alive and well now," Henri responded.

Ava put her croissant down, horrified. "You don't think something has happened to him?"

"No. But we're only confirming what we know."

Ava breathed a sigh of relief. "What did you learn?"

"Luc's in love with Bea and wants her to leave Yves," Henri said.

Ava's eyes widened. "Jealousy. That's a classic motive. Was Luc the one who tried to kill Yves?"

Henri shook his head no. "If Yves dies, he'll become a martyr in Bea's mind. Luc needs a Yves who is alive and well, so Bea can divorce him. There's also the property. The abbey is owned by a holding in Luxembourg. The apartment near Luxembourg Gardens belongs to Bea. She inherited it from her parents. She took out a huge loan using it as collateral when Yves inherited the abbey."

"To help him fix it up?"

Henri shrugged. "Perhaps. The thing is there is a large payment coming up..."

"So Bea needs money."

Henri nodded.

"What would all this mean if Yves died?" Ava asked.

"It depends on many factors. If there was life insurance, Bea might be better off with Yves dead. Then again, depending on how the holding is set up, she might be worse off if he died. Again, I wasn't able to discover a lot on the holding. I asked someone I know in Luxembourg to look into it. I'm waiting to hear back."

Ava knew that property and money were important issues in France. In a country that didn't like to talk about money, it was always below the surface. As a former notary, no one knew the ins and outs of the question like Henri.

"Even if Bea might benefit financially from Yves's death, I don't see her as a murderer. She still loves him. That doesn't mean someone else didn't do it to help her out."

"Who?" Ava asked.

"Hard to say. There's something else that puzzled me. I'm sure Luc recognized me from a conference we both went to years ago. Yet, he didn't mention it. I'm going down to the abbey with Bea and Luc this afternoon. If Yves is alive, I suspect he'll be there. Plus, we can't forget that he asked me to look at his books. There must be a reason for that."

"I'm sure the seminar is in the abbey. There's a train from the Gare de Lyon station this afternoon at five," Ava said, defensive.

Henri nodded and didn't speak.

Ava stiffened her spine and launched into the argument she had prepared. "I have to go to the abbey. It's important. In some ways, I do feel that I was chosen. From the dark-haired stranger to the "you are a special person" flyer, the universe chose me to save Yves's life. Henri, even if you say no, I'm going to go," she said, taking care not to mention today's horoscope.

"On the contrary," Henri said. "That's a splendid idea."

Ava was so astonished she could barely speak. "My going to the abbey is a good idea?" she asked, wary.

"Absolutely. That way if someone does try to kill you, I'll be nearby," Henri said with a chuckle.

"That's not funny."

Suddenly serious, Henri shook his head. "I'm not joking. Yves is in danger. We don't know why, but we do know that there's no smoke without fire. Let's not forget that you might have seen his would-be killer."

Ava fell silent. In all the detective books she had read, the person who had seen the killer was usually the next to die.

Henri poured the last of the coffee in Ava's cup. "Remember, when we meet there. We don't know each other."

"Do you miss my uncle?" Ava asked as she finished off her second croissant.

Henri sighed. "I'd hoped that Sext and DeAth would last longer than it did. But it wasn't to be. Since I inherited you, in a certain sense, it is continuing."

"What would my uncle have done in this case?"

My French way of sleuthing wasn't always his cup of tea. He would look at the people involved and study them."

"Did it work?"

"Sometimes yes. Sometimes no."

"What would you do?"

"Follow the money or the heart," Henri said. "Or both.

CHAPTER 11

With plenty of time before her train left, Ava pedaled a *Velib'* bike along the left bank of the Seine River toward the Gare de Lyon train station. Her overnight bag was stuffed into the bike's front basket. As she rode past the outdoor sculptures that dotted the riverbank, she heard a lion roar in the zoo in the nearby botanical gardens, the Jardin des Plantes. She had a vague memory of reading that starving Parisians had eaten the zoo animals during the French Revolution.

While that had nothing to do with the situation at hand, it certainly showed that Parisians were resourceful. If Yves's would-be murderer was a Parisian, she would need to be just as resourceful.

Five minutes later, she sped across the Seine, zipped through the blocked traffic on the opposite quay and raced up the street to the entrance of the Gare de Lyon train station. Trains for central and southeast France, Switzerland and Italy left from there.

Paris also had the Gare de Nord, *nord* meaning north. Trains heading north and northwest to Amsterdam left from that station, while trains heading east and northeast to Germany and Strasbourg left from the Gare de l'Est, *est* meaning east. Logically, the Gare de Lyon should have been called the Gare de Sud, as *sud* meant south. However, the station was named after a large city in the center east of France. To confuse things even more, Paris also had the Gare de Montparnasse, the Gare d'Austerlitz and the Gare Saint-Lazare train stations, which, in her opinion, destroyed any clarity the system had.

Not to mention the Gare d'Orsay, which had become an art museum.

Ava zigzagged in and out of traffic until she saw the train station clock tower looming high in the air. Some compared the clock tower to Big Ben in London. The very essence of her Britishness bristled at the idea that people could imagine for an instant that the two towers were similar.

Big Ben was Big Ben.

The clock tower in the Gare de Lyon was just a clock tower.

Glancing up at the time, she saw she had thirty minutes

before her train left. She had already purchased her ticket online so she had plenty of time to spare. After zooming around a stopped bus, she wheeled to the right and braked sharply at the *Velib'* bike station. Her eyes scanned the bike rack looking for an empty spot. Seeing a lone space between two bikes at the end, she beamed.

Luck was with her.

She walked her bike over, lifted it up and pushed it into the empty space. The light on the stand flashed from an orangey red to green. This was followed by two quick beeps, indicating that the bike was registered as returned.

She grabbed her overnight bag and slung it over her shoulder. She strode toward the station entrance, slowing only to check her reflection in the window of a parked car.

Studying it, she wondered if she looked like the type of person about to embark on a long spiritual weekend. However, the face that gazed back at her was exactly the same pre-spiritual face she had always had.

From what she could see, her presence at last night's lecture and her subsequent dip in the canal, a kind of baptism, had not changed a thing. Ava defiantly swiped on more red lipstick. Spiritual pilgrim or not, this was France. Certain standards existed. She pulled her hair off her face, twisting the long strands into a makeshift chignon and nodded in approval. She now looked like someone who was ready to become a master of the universe.

Satisfied that her new look would pass muster, Ava, dressed simply in jeans, a black T-shirt and an old suede jacket that she had purchased at a Parisian flea market, a jacket that had come with a ticket stub for a 1973 rock concert in its pocket, made her way up the winding driveway, ignoring the honking cars and taxis that were stuck in traffic.

Inside the station, it was pure chaos. It was as if all of Paris had decided to take advantage of the long weekend to flee the city.

Ava stopped in a shop to buy a candy bar for the train ride. While waiting in line, she scrutinized the man in line before her. Now that she was a sleuth, she needed to up her game on describing people.

The man was wearing blue jeans, beat up slip-on skate shoes, a grey T-shirt and a navy-blue hoodie sweatshirt. He had a candid face, short hair and wore small round glasses. Ava guessed that he was twenty-six or twenty-seven. There was nothing that gave any clues as to his profession. If forced to choose, Ava would go for a doctoral student in biology. Like her, he had a small bag flung over his shoulder. However, his bag had a "Save the Polar Bears" sticker on it that showed he was environmentally conscious.

Trying to guess his height was harder.

She estimated that he was just a bit taller than she was.

To verify this, she edged toward him. As she lined her shoulder up with his, he turned and eyed her with astonishment.

As coolly as could be, she stepped past him to the cash register and paid for her candy bar. When she had finished paying, the man was gone.

Ava sidled her way through the crowd and entered the main hall. She halted in front of the enormous electronic board that hung from station ceiling. It would soon show the platform her train left from.

She glanced around. No one from last night's lecture was in sight. There was no sign of Lili and Arnaud. Ava didn't doubt they would be on the train.

Nibbling on her candy bar, Ava waited. Exactly fifteen minutes before her train's departure, its destination lit up in white lights on the board, followed by the platform number.

With a sense of excitement, Ava headed toward the platform. When she reached it, she noticed the "Save the Polar Bears" man standing there with a frown.

Recognizing her from the store, the man smiled. "Is this the right platform for this stop?" he asked in an American accent as he showed her his ticket.

Ava checked his destination. They were both going to the same place.

She handed his ticket back to him. "You're at the right

platform. You need to validate your ticket by punching it in the machine."

The man followed her over to the machine. He validated his ticket after she validated hers. He then followed her down the platform and onto the train. For a moment, she feared he was going to pester her. Instead, he walked to the far end of the car.

As there was no reserved seating, Ava grabbed the first free seat she saw. Sliding into it, she saw the couple from the canal, Lili and Arnaud, walk down the aisle. She slumped down, hoping they wouldn't see her. As she did this, she realized it made no sense at all.

The couple would certainly notice her when she got off the train and went to the abbey with them. To her regret, they also sat at the far end of the train, too far away for her to overhear their conversation.

When the train pulled away, it was half-empty. It was only a local train going to the outskirts of Paris. It wasn't a high-speed train that would whisk you to the south of France and the blue waters of the Mediterranean.

Settling in for the ride, Ava pulled out a notebook. While her invisible notebook was fine for jotting down a few notes, it had become clear to Ava that in a case of life and death, she needed a real notebook to write things down. Pen in hand, she turned her mind to her list of suspects.

So far, the list was short.

Suspect 1: Bea, Yves's wife.

Yves had had affairs. He had gone missing and had not informed his wife he was alive. Perhaps he was afraid of her. However, he had left a letter inviting Sext and DeAth to appraise his books. If he was truly afraid of his wife, he wouldn't have wanted her to know he was alive.

Suspect 2: Luc, the family friend and lawyer. Luc was in love with Bea and hoped to marry her. While Henri had all but ruled Luc out, Ava couldn't eliminate him until she had met him in person. Maybe she'd read too many murder mysteries, but the lover always had a motive.

Suspect 3: Kris, the earth mother. Kris had believed Yves was dead until she spoke with him. Whether that put Kris high or low on the list of suspects, Ava had no idea. What was clear was that Kris was a true believer. Ava found the phone call story fishy.

Suspect 4: Margot. If Kris was to be believed, Margot had a crush on Yves, a crush that was unreciprocated. Did that mean she'd want to kill him? Perhaps… But before the lecture, it was clear that Margot thought Yves was alive. However, that might be a ruse.

Suspects 5 & 6: Lili and Arnaud. Of all the suspects, they were the two who intrigued Ava the most.

Lili was sure that Yves was dead and seemed certain that

Arnaud knew something about the death. She had almost insinuated that he was implicated in it.

On the other hand, Arnaud believed that Yves was alive and was playing some game. Arnaud had feelings for Lili. Did Lili love Yves? Did Yves love Lili? If so, that would add an unexpected twist to an increasingly complicated tale.

Finally, there was the young man with the flyer. In a certain way, it was he, not the universe, who had chosen Ava as a special person. You could say that he was acting as an agent for the universe or that she really was a special person. However, he had pretended not to recognize her at the lecture, and she had seen him at the canal.

Could he be the one who had pushed her?

Ava thought back to the expression on his face as he gazed down at her. He had looked worried and concerned. He didn't have the triumphant look of a would-be assassin. Ava put him on her "*wait and see*" list.

And then there was Matt or Max, whoever he was... Ava suspected she would soon meet him.

.

CHAPTER 12

When the train entered the station, there were only four people left in the car. Ava remained in her seat until the American man and the couple had left. Slinging her bag over her shoulder, she walked down the aisle, climbed down the metal steps onto the platform and followed the trio out of the station at a distance.

Walking to the exit, she wondered what Henri had learned on his drive down from Paris with Bea and Luc. They had left Paris an hour earlier. Unless traffic was horrible, they should have arrived at the abbey by now. She also wondered how she was going to explain her presence at the seminar.

Improvisation, Ava… Improvisation.

But as she had never been good at improvisation, she was worried.

Outside the station, the American man was standing by

himself. Frowning, he glanced around as if looking for someone or something. Lili and Arnaud were standing on the other side of the entrance, deep in a heated discussion. Arnaud was doing most of the talking, while Lili listened stone-faced. Ava strode to a timetable on the wall behind them in a bold attempt to hear what they were saying.

The moment she walked past them, she felt eyes bearing down on her. Looking up, she saw Lili staring at her. As casually as possible, Ava ran her finger down the timetable.

Just then, a white passenger van roared up, honking loudly. It braked in front of Ava and the couple. Without hesitating, the couple headed to the van.

A tall bald-headed man in his forties hopped out of the van. He was wearing jeans, muddy boots and a blue plaid shirt. "Sorry I'm late," the man said to the couple as he walked around the van. He slid the passenger door open for them.

Ava watched the goings-on without moving.

The bald-headed man looked familiar.

It was the old "familiar stranger" concept at work again.

She might have seen the man anywhere. The only thing she knew was that she hadn't seen him at the lecture last night.

"I hate to keep bothering you. Are you here for the seminar?" the American man asked as he walked over.

Turning, she noticed that his glasses were broken and were taped in the corner. It was becoming clearer and clearer that Yves was not in this for the money. If you were going to fleece your flock, you need to choose a flock with fleece.

Shifting her bag on her shoulder, Ava smiled. "Yes, I am. I believe the van is for us," she said, pointing at the waiting vehicle.

The American relaxed. "Thanks. I was afraid I might have come to the wrong place. I'm Steve Warren."

"Ava Sext," she responded. "You're American?"

Steve nodded. "From San Francisco. You're from England?"

"London. But I live in Paris."

"The accent gave you away." Steve waved his hand at the van. "After you…"

Walking in front of him, Ava was puzzled.

What was he doing here?

Steve didn't seem like a spiritual seeker, and he certainly didn't look like a chosen one. Just as her mind was about to gallop ahead and conjure up hundreds of reasons for Steve's presence, she heard her late Uncle Charles's voice in the back of her mind:

"Don't jump to conclusions, Ava. Too often, we base our opinions on the past. But today is a new day. Yesterday is over. And the present very rarely resembles the past. It's not that lessons can't be learned. They can. But take it slowly."

Her uncle was right.

All she knew for certain was that Yves was in danger.

As for spiritual seekers?

Ava had almost zero experience with seeking spiritual truth. Her parents had gone to church on Christmas and Easter and for baptisms, weddings and deaths. She had gone with them until she was old enough to opt out. Her only other experience with spiritual seeking had been a few sessions with a Ouija board at summer camp. She had also been a vegetarian from nineteen to twenty although that didn't really count as a spiritual experience. Guiltily, she thought of the roasted organic chicken with garlic she had eaten for lunch. She sighed. Not everyone was cut out to save the planet.

The bald-headed man frowned when Ava and Steve walked up to the van. He removed a paper from his pocket. "And you are?"

The American smiled. "Steve Warren,"

The bald-headed man ran his finger down the paper. He puckered his lips in annoyance. "You're not my list. Your name, miss?"

"Ava Sext. I don't know if Yves added me to the list. I wasn't sure that I could come."

The bald-headed man sighed. He took out a pen and wrote Steve and Ava's names on the paper. "Get in the van. I'm going to check to see if the people who are on my list aren't wandering around the station lost."

When Steve and Ava reached the van's passenger door, Ava noticed that Lili was staring at her oddly from the interior.

Lili narrowed her eyes. "You know Yves? I don't remember you from the lectures."

She's lying, Ava thought. She stared right at me last night.

Sitting next to Lili, Arnaud eyed Ava. A look of recognition spread across his face. "I remember you," he said with an inviting grin. He turned to Lili. "She couldn't find the entrance to the lecture last night."

Lili relaxed slightly. "I don't understand why Yves doesn't put a map on the flyer. I'm sure there are people who never find their way in.

"Then they must not be chosen ones," Ava said, half-joking.

Lili and Arnaud laughed. Steve looked puzzled.

"When did you last see Yves?" Lili asked Ava.

For a brief instant, Ava considered saying that she had seen him after his disappearance in Italy. However, given Lili's animosity toward her that would be like poking an angry bear.

Ava shrugged. "I don't remember. Maybe a month ago. I met Yves at an antiquarian bookstore in Paris. He mentioned the seminar and said if I came through Paris at the time, I should come."

Astonished, Steve raised his eyebrows. Ava remembered that she had told him she lived in Paris.

Now it was Arnaud's turn to be puzzled. "How did you know about last night's lecture? It was only announced at the last minute."

"Believe it or not, I saw a flyer on a streetlight. Pure synchronicity," Ava answered.

Lili nodded. "Yves believed in synchronicity."

"Yves believes in a lot of things," Arnaud replied cryptically with a sharp glance at Lili.

When the bald-headed man reappeared from the station, Steve and Ava climbed into the back of the van. They sat in the far row of seats behind Lili and Arnaud. Grumbling to himself, the bald-headed man walked around the van and pulled the passenger door closed. He then went to the driver's seat, hopped into it, and turned on the motor. He swirled his head around.

"For those who don't know me, I'm Maximilien. Max, for short."

Max! Ava had found her missing man.

"This is Lili and Arnaud," Max said, introducing the couple behind him. "Who are not on my list either..."

"Has Yves arrived?" Lili asked, anxious.

"Not to my knowledge," Max said.

Lili's face fell.

"Where are the others?" Ava asked. Last night, Lili had spoken about the inner circle, and Max had a list of people to pick up.

Max shook his head as he buckled his seatbelt. "I have no idea. I came here to pick up seven people on my list. Instead, I'm leaving with four who aren't on it. The sooner Yves comes back, the better."

Astonished, Steve leaned forward. "Yves won't be here?"

"The only person who knows when Yves will appear is Yves," Max said philosophically as he pulled away.

Lili turned and studied Steve. "You didn't hear about Yves's disappearance?"

Steve's astonishment turned to pure alarm. "Disappearance? When? How?"

"Three weeks ago," Arnaud answered.

Steve let out a deep breath. His expression changed. He appeared calmer. "No. I didn't know."

He's spoken to Yves since then, Ava thought. Before she could rein in her imagination, it went galloping off. *Steve had come to see Yves about something, maybe even something secret.* However, looking at Steve's taped glasses and hoodie, she couldn't imagine what that might be.

"Disappearance only means no one knows where you are. Yves knows where he is. He isn't missing," Max stated, matter-of-factly.

Ava couldn't agree more. In fact, Yves had looked very alive when she had seen him. With a sigh, she crossed Steve off her list of suspects. Steve hadn't known about Yves's disappearance. He was here because Yves had invited him after the so-called disappearance. While Steve was no longer a suspect in her eyes, his presence proved Henri right... *Yves would be at the abbey.*

A shiver ran up Ava's spine, and her heart began to beat faster. Normally, it was the criminal who returned to the scene of the crime. In this case, it was the victim who was coming to the scene of his death unless she and Henri could stop it.

As Max pulled the van onto the main road, he eyed Lili in the rear view mirror. "What treats did you bring for us this time?"

Lili smiled. "You'll see tonight at dinner."

"Lili is a pastry chef," Arnaud explained to Steve and Ava.

"Yves lives for her pastries," Max said as he drove through town. "He says they're as sweet as she is."

Ava looked at Arnaud. The vein in his neck had begun to throb.

"What do you do?" Lili asked Ava.

"I create custom book collections for book collectors," Ava answered. It wasn't really a lie as a collector had asked Henri to create a collection for him, and Henri had asked Ava to help.

Steve eyed her strangely. "You're an expert on books?"

"I wouldn't say I'm an expert," Ava replied modestly. "I just love working with them. What do you do?"

"As little as possible," Steve joked. "And even that tires me out."

"I agree!" Arnaud said, chuckling. "We spend too much time working. When I'm not slacking off, I'm a graphic artist."

Steve peered at Max. "Are we far from the abbey?"

"Twenty minutes with traffic. As there's never any traffic we'll be there in fifteen," Max said, laughing at his own joke.

Ava noticed that Steve had avoided telling anyone what he did for a living.

The van sped along a deserted country road and then entered a thick forest. Every now and then, the late afternoon sun burst through the tall trees, casting dancing beams of light on the van's windows.

"I've never been in this part of France," Steve confessed. "It's prettier than I'd imagined."

"You're in for a treat. The abbey and its grounds are beautiful," Max said like a proud father.

"Max is lucky enough to have lived at the abbey for years. He worked with the former owner," Arnaud explained.

Yves's uncle, Ava thought.

At the top of a hill, Max slowed the van. "That's the abbey

down below."

Looking down, Ava saw a grayish white stone edifice in ruins. Only its walls were standing. They soared high in the air. Strangely, this gave the edifice even more power.

"The manor house where you'll be staying is next to the abbey," Max said. "Don't worry. The manor house has a roof."

As the van sped down the steep hill toward the abbey, everyone was silent. Arnaud stared out the window, tight-jawed. Lili looked worried and was biting her lip. Even the usually chatty Max had stopped speaking. His eyes were glued to the road. Picking up on the vibes in the van, Steve was tense. Ava had the feeling that something was about to happen.

At the bottom of the hill, the van veered left down a narrow road that had a "Private Property" sign posted at its entrance. The van advanced slowly down the rutted dirt road.

"We had a wet spring. The rain wreaked havoc on the road. Six weeks ago, the creek flooded its banks for the first time in years. Water was everywhere. You remember that, don't you, Lili?" Max asked as he maneuvered the van around a hole in the road.

Arnaud stiffened and eyed Lili. "You were here six weeks ago? You didn't mention that..."

Lili but her lower lip. "Kris had a few of us come up on a Saturday."

"No one asked me," Arnaud said to no one in particular.

Lili didn't respond.

The van went around a bend and came out into a large open plain that had a creek running across it. The ghostlike abbey was on the creek's far side. A small group of people was standing at the edge of a creek.

Max swore under his breath. "What in the name of heaven?"

As the van drew closer, Ava saw that the group was composed of Henri, Bea and Luc. They were standing next to a car that was stuck in the mud. A wooden bridge was behind them.

Max stopped next to the trio. Max, Arnaud and Steve climbed out and walked over to help them. As Ava was pretending not to know Henri, she stayed in the van with Lili.

Lili stared out the window, worried. "Something's wrong with the bridge."

The minute Max reached her, Bea lit into him, furious. "Max, some boards in the bridge gave way when Luc drove onto it. If he hadn't gunned the car back, we'd be in the creek."

His face reddening, Max stared at the bridge. He strode over to it and inspected it from all angles. He walked back to Bea, shaking his head. "I warned Yves. That bridge was an accident waiting to happen."

"And now it has," Bea responded. "Fortunately, no one was hurt."

"Can we get my car out of the mud?" Luc asked, pointing at the vehicle.

"First, let's get your things. You can come with us in the van. I'll pull the car out later with the tractor," Max said with a sigh.

The men helped the trio carry their belongings to the van. When everyone was seated, Max gunned its motor and drove off without a word. Bea took charge of the introductions.

"I'm Bea, Yves's wife. This is Luc Gault and Mr. DeAth."

Lili stared at Bea, astonished.

From her expression, Ava guessed that this was the first time Lili had met Bea.

Henri smiled at everyone. "Please call me Henri."

Doing her best to pretend she didn't know him, Ava smiled back. "I'm Ava."

"Steve," Steve said with a nod.

"Arnaud and Lili," Arnaud added.

Max drove down a dirt road that ran alongside the creek. The abbey was to their right. It was even more impressive close up. It had a mysterious majesty to it, a majesty that was untouched by time. When he reached an old stone bridge, Max slowed the van and turned right onto it. As they drove over the creek, Ava looked down at its high waters and remembered her horoscope:

You will cross distant waters and be tested. Failure will be fatal.

CHAPTER 13

The van drove down a rutted road on the other side of the
ruined abbey. The ruts were so deep that several times the van
got stuck. Each time, Max would sigh, shift gears, back up and
start off again.

"Believe it or not, this is the best road to the abbey," Max
said with a guffaw after extricating the van from a deep rut.
"You're probably lucky the bridge gave way, Bea. Even if you
had made it over it, without a four-wheel drive like Yves, you'd
be stuck in the mud."

"Where is the Jeep?" Bea asked.

"Right where Yves left it. In the manor house garage,"
Max replied.

"Why didn't you come to the lecture last night, Max?"
Arnaud asked out of the blue.

Max's face clouded over. "The abbey needs ten people like me working here. Unfortunately, there's just me."

When the van reached the end of the abbey, it sped up. Max came to a halt in front of a long two-story building made of the same grayish white stone as the abbey. He honked twice, jumped out and walked around to open the van's passenger door.

"Why they call this the manor house is beyond me," Bea said as she climbed out, shaking her limbs awake.

As the others clambered out behind her, the manor house's front door swung open and Kris stepped out. A look of surprise appeared on her face when she saw the van's passengers who were collecting their belongings. In disbelief, she turned to Max.

"What's going on? Where are the others," she asked.

Max shrugged. "The people on the list weren't at the station. These four were," he said waving at Steve, Ava, Lili and Arnaud. "I found Bea and her friends next to the bridge. Part of it gave way when they drove over it. They nearly ended up in the creek."

"The creek?" Kris repeated, frowning.

"I'll use the tractor to pull their car out of the mud tomorrow," Max said.

When Bea strode up to the door, Kris turned confrontational. Crossing her arms, she blocked Bea's way. "I didn't know you were coming. If you'd called, I would have told you there was no room."

Bea stared straight through Kris. "I'll be staying in Yves's quarters. My guests can stay in the red and blue rooms."

Kris didn't move. "You can't stay here, Bea. We're holding a seminar."

Not the least bit intimidated, Bea stared Kris down. "We'll be staying until tomorrow evening. We'll be joining you for dinner."

Kris lowered her voice. "You can't order me around like that," she snarled.

Amused, Bea smiled at her. "The abbey is mine. I can do whatever I want with it."

Kris frowned, bewildered. "The abbey belongs to a holding in Luxembourg."

Bea nodded. "A holding I control. Who knows, I may even sell it one day."

"Yves won't allow it," Kris protested.

"My husband has little say in the matter," Bea responded, putting emphasis on the word "husband". She turned to Henri. "Once you've settled in your rooms, I'll give you a tour of the abbey. Luc has already visited it, but he's welcome to join us."

"I prefer to putter around the library," Luc replied.

Without missing a beat, Ava turned to Bea. "Could I join you? This is my first time here."

Bea hesitated and then smiled graciously. "Of course. We'll meet in the entrance in twenty minutes. Would anyone else like to come?"

Steve shook his head. "Another time perhaps."

"We've seen it, thank you," Lili responded.

Ill at ease, Max shifted from foot to foot, eyeing Kris. "What do you want me to do?"

Exasperated by the situation, Kris stepped aside. "Show them their rooms and then come help me with dinner."

"Has everyone got their belongings?" Max asked, examining the group in front of him.

The group followed Max into a large entrance hall and up a flight of steps. The bedrooms were distributed down two sides of a long hallway. Half of the rooms gave onto a flowering back garden. The other half overlooked the front of the building where the van was parked.

"These rooms were used by hunting parties. Fortunately, they're more comfortable today than they were back then," Max announced as he slowed and opened a door. The bedroom, done up in various shades of red, overlooked the front of the house. "You can stay here, Luc."

Luc went in and closed the door behind him.

Max opened the door next to Luc's room. "The blue room is yours, Henri. You've lucked out. It has the most comfortable bed in the whole house." As Henri entered the room, Max threw open four doors that gave onto the back garden. "Take your pick," he said to the others.

Without hesitating, Ava entered the room directly in front of her. The bedroom had a four-poster bed with a white chintz cover on it. The room also had a comfortable armchair and a reading light. A small bookshelf in the corner of the room was filled with classics. She nodded with approval. Books always made her feel at home. Remembering that she only had twenty minutes, she freshened up as quickly as possible and put on some red lipstick.

She placed her clothing on the long bench at the end of the bed. She walked over to the door. There was no key and no way for her to lock it. After hesitating, she threw her wallet and phone into the pocket of her jacket. She hid her notebook under the cushions of the armchair.

Before leaving, she glanced out the window at the garden below. To her astonishment, someone was lurking in the shrubbery. When the person stepped out into the open, she recognized the young man who had given her the flyer in Paris. In a flash, Ava was out of her room and down the stairs. By the time she reached the garden, the man was gone. Steve was standing there looking at the bushes.

"Did you see anyone?" Ava asked.

"No," Steve said quickly, too quickly. He turned and entered the house.

Intrigued, Ava watched him leave.

Had the man been waiting for Steve?

Alone in the garden, Ava poked around the bushes. The man had been there. He wasn't a figment of her imagination.

As she passed near open French doors at the far end of the garden, she heard loud voices coming from inside. Creeping over, she stepped behind a flowering wisteria bush to listen. She immediately identified the voices. They belonged to Kris and Max.

"Bea can't stay here. I won't allow it. We have to do something, Max," Kris said.

Ava inched forward until she could see inside. The two were in a small office. Max was standing near the door, while Kris paced back and forth like a caged lion. She was so angry that she was shaking.

"I don't see how you're going to stop her. Bea is Yves's wife," Max said calmly.

"They married years ago. She means nothing to him."

Listening to Kris, Ava wondered if Kris was in love with Yves, too. If so, the field was getting crowded.

"They've been married for twenty years. That counts for something," Max replied.

"I've devoted my whole life to the work. I won't let her sell the abbey," Kris said, balling up her fists.

"Bea just said that to get your goat. She may hold the power, but she would never go against Yves's wishes," Max said. He paused and eyed Kris. "Did you really talk to him?"

"Of course, I did," she snapped.

"Then he's not dead?"

"If he were dead, I wouldn't have been able to speak with him!" Kris exclaimed.

With a worried look, Max stared straight at Kris. "When did Yves say he was coming?"

Evasive, Kris looked away. "This weekend. But you know Yves. He'll appear when he wants to appear and not a moment before."

"Maybe then he'll tell us why he disappeared in Italy. He should have let us know he was OK. Unless..."

Kris squinted her eyes. "Unless what?"

Max knitted his brow. "Unless he's afraid."

"Afraid of what?"

"I don't know," Max said in a tone that implied he did know.

"What are you trying to say? That someone tried to kill him?"

"I'm not saying anything. I just don't like what's going on. I don't like the fact that Yves has disappeared," he said. Overcome with emotion, he sank into a chair. "What will we do if we have to leave the abbey?"

Defiant, Kris crossed her arms over her chest. "We won't leave. The work is linked to the abbey. Anyone knows that."

"The work can be done anywhere."

"With Yves perhaps. But if he doesn't want to continue, we'll need the abbey," Kris said.

"He never said he'd abandon the work. Don't start imagining things."

"Who's the young man with the new woman?" Kris asked, changing the subject.

"He's American. His name is Steve. Yves invited him a while ago."

"Did you learn anything about the woman?"

"Ava? She works in books. She met Yves at some bookshop."

Kris frowned. "Books? Did she say anything else?"

"No. Are we still holding the seminar?"

"Of course. Nothing else is important. The work must go on. I don't understand where the others are. But these four people are here. It's not an accident. The universe wants them here."

Flush-faced, Margot appeared in the doorway. "I know why the others didn't come."

Kris and Max turned. They stared at her.

"Yves emailed them and cancelled the seminar," Margot said.

"Yves? That's impossible," Kris replied before falling silent.

"Impossible? Yves does what he wants to do," Max said, rising to his feet. "That's our fault. We let him do it."

Margot looked at Max, bewildered. "What do you mean?"

"Kris is right. Yves isn't the work. Yet since he's come to the abbey, the work rises and shines on Yves's moods and desires," Max said.

A strange look appeared on Margot's face. "What if Yves didn't cancel the seminar?"

"If he didn't, who did?" Kris asked.

"Anyone of us could have hacked into Yves's account," Margot replied.

"How could we possibly do that?" Max asked.

"His password is saved on the computer. That's how I got into it."

Max stepped toward her. "What else did you learn?"

"No other emails have been sent since Italy," Margot replied. "The email cancelling the seminar was sent late last night. She turned to Kris. "Yves didn't mention cancelling when you spoke to him?"

"No," Kris said. "But we only spoke for a few seconds."

"It's easy to solve. We'll ask him when he appears," Max said.

"If he appears," Margot said in an odd strangled voice and

left the room.

Feeling a presence behind her. Ava jumped and turned. It was Henri.

"Did you hear that?" Ava whispered.

Henri nodded. He looked worried.

Before Ava could add that she had seen the young man with the flyer, Bea stepped out into the garden and waved at them.

"I was looking for you. Let's go to the abbey while it's still light."

Henri and Ava crossed the garden toward her. As they walked, Ava felt eyes drilling into her back. Glancing back, she saw Max staring.

It was not a friendly stare.

CHAPTER 14

Light trickled through the gothic window openings in the whitish gray stone walls of the ruined abbey. As Bea, Henri and Ava ambled through the ghostlike edifice ravaged by time, Bea gave a running dialogue on the building's origins.

"The abbey was built in the late fourteenth century by Cistercian monks. One hundred years, they abandoned it to move to a richer abbey in the north. It stayed in the order's hands until the late sixteenth century when a wealthy local family bought it. They used the woods for hunting and eventually built the manor house. By the time my husband's great uncle bought it, the abbey was in ruins. He fell under the its spell and spent vast sums to bring it back to its former glory, depleting the family fortune. His son, my husband's uncle, also devoted his life to restoring the abbey. Although I have no idea how he found the money to do that. When Yves inherited it, he, too, fell in love with the abbey and spent even more money on it, my money…"

"The building is captivating," Henri said. "It has a special purity to it."

Lagging behind Bea and Henri but close enough to hear their conversation, Ava couldn't agree with Henri more. Even if she hadn't been a chosen one, walking through the abbey made her feel that she had a special connection to something much larger.

"People in the region believe the abbey's haunted. Some say it's cursed. To be honest, I don't like coming here. If Yves hadn't wanted you to see his books, I wouldn't have come," Bea admitted.

"Do you really intend to sell it?" Henri asked.

Bea laughed. "Keeping or selling the abbey is Yves's decision." Walking up to a huge capstone, Bea slowed. "Later tonight, we'll watch the light show. You'll see how the abbey used to look."

Puzzled, Henri frowned.

"As it was too expensive to rebuild all the walls, Yves had a lighting expert come and install lights and special effects. At night, they give you the illusion that the abbey is intact. It was a wonderful idea. Yves is very creative," Bea said in admiration. Suddenly anxious, she turned to Henri. "You're sure he's alive?"

With a reassuring smile, Henri nodded. "I'm sure. How

else could he have sent me the letter?"

For a moment, Bea appeared sad. "I love Yves. I'm just tired after all these years. The women... I've gotten used to them. For the past ten years, we've lived separate lives. Despite that, I always felt he was my partner. But since he inherited the abbey and decided to become a guru, he's turned into someone I don't know."

"And Luc?" Henri asked.

Bea's expression softened. "I intend to spend the future with him. To do that, I have to break with Yves."

Eavesdropping, Ava wondered what Bea meant when she said that Yves had become a guru. As if he could read Ava's thoughts, Henri eyed Bea.

"What did you mean by Yves became a guru?" he asked.

Ava took her phone out and began snapping photos of the abbey, stepping closer and closer to Bea and Henri to overhear everything being said.

"Since he started "the work" as he calls it, everyone is in awe of him. They've elevated him to an almost godlike status. The Yves I married had a strong ego. The Yves who exists today is pure ego. That's not an admirable quality in anyone." Bea ran her hand over the large capstone. "Some people love old stones. I love them, too. But I absolutely hate these. I hate them even more because of what came with them..."

Henri raised his eyebrows waiting for her to continue.

"He inherited the group when he inherited the abbey. Back then, the group was tiny. It was just Kris, Max, Margot and a few other believers. They all treat Yves as if he's the messiah. The worst is he believes it himself," Bea said. "If Yves were the messiah, I'd know it... He even told me before he left for Italy that he could beat death."

"How does he intend to do that?" Henri asked, stupefied.

Bea laughed. "I'm not a chosen one, I can't tell you that."

Ava was confused. If Yves really believed he could beat death, he wouldn't be worried about someone killing him, and he wouldn't have gone into hiding.

"Let's go into the main space while there's still light," Bea said to both Ava and Henri.

Ava took a few more photos and then followed them into the abbey's central section. It was a large solemn space. Its far wall rose high into the air. Ivy covered most of it. Here and there, thin saplings grew from the broken stone floor. The intrusion of nature added to the abbey's sense of infinite solitude.

"Yves's cousin said he'd seen ghosts here. What I see is a money pit." Bea pointed to the far wall. "Water from the creek is destabilizing it. It needs to be shored up or it might come tumbling down. In my opinion, that might not be a bad thing."

Henri spun around to take in the vastness of the space. "It's magnificent. I can understand why Yves wants to preserve it."

"Yves can do whatever he wants, but I need my money back. And if that means selling the abbey, that's what he'll have to do." Bea shook her head. "Yves is resourceful. He'll find a way. Before he left for Italy, he assured me that he would get the money."

"There's something that puzzles me. Why didn't Yves put a member of the group in charge of the holding rather than you?" Henri questioned.

"We may have our differences, but Yves trusts me implicitly. I would never do anything he didn't agree with." Bea looked up at the fading light. "I suggest I show you the library before dinner. That's why we're here." She turned to Ava. "If you wait another ten or fifteen minutes, the setting sun will come through the window frames and light up the opposite wall. The people who built the abbey were true artists."

"Thanks. I will wait," Ava said as she continued to take photos. Watching them walk off, Ava sat down on a large chunk of stone. There was something peaceful about the abbey. As the minutes ticked by, she began to feel uneasy. It wasn't anything she could put her finger on. It worried her enough to stand up and look all around her.

Just as the sun came streaming through the windows, lighting up the opposite wall, something caught Ava's attention at the far end of the abbey.

Someone was moving across it.

Ava sprinted off up toward the person, taking care to remain in the shadows.

When she reached the large arch that separated the space she was in from a smaller space, she saw Steve striding through the abbey. He walked to a side wall and slipped out through an opening.

Ava waited a few seconds and then ran after him. When she went through opening in the wall, there was no sign of Steve.

Frowning, she scanned the area around her. There were some low ruined stone buildings nearby. There was also a thick forest of oak and beech trees. Turning, she saw Steve standing nervously at the forest's edge.

Ava hid, waiting to see who would appear. As the minutes ticked by, Steve became more and more agitated.

Was he waiting for Yves?

Maybe he was waiting for the young man...

Something struck Ava. The Steve standing near the forest was a man whose entire body oozed purpose. He was not a slacker who did as little as possible as he had implied in the van.

For one brief instant, Ava wondered if he had come to kill Yves. Remembering his "Save the Polar Bears" bag and taped glasses, she immediately discarded the theory.

Steve was not a murderer.

However, everything indicated that he had been in contact with Yves since his disappearance and had come to the abbey for a specific purpose that she needed to discover.

To her disappointment, no one came to meet Steve. Visibly disappointed, he turned and retraced his steps through the dark abbey. Ava followed him at a distance. Whoever he was going to meet hadn't appeared. Ava didn't know if that was good or bad, but she intended to find out.

CHAPTER 15

Ava crossed through the manor house's back garden. Flowering bushes and tall trees lined its outer edges. As she walked, she heard a loud rustling in the bushes.

She stopped and eyed the shrubbery, her every sense on alert.

Someone was there.

She wasn't alone.

Before fear paralyzed her, she stepped toward the bushes. "Is anyone there?"

Silence was the only response.

Unable to shake the feeling that someone was watching her, she edged closer to the dark trees. "Mr. Dubois, is that you?"

Silence.

Suddenly, there was movement in the bushes. This was followed by the sound of running feet.

Ava didn't wait to see who it was. In a flash, she turned and was sprinting to the manor house. If the devil had been behind her, she couldn't have run any faster. When she reached the house, she pulled opened the door, stepped inside and slammed it closed behind her. She leaned against it, her heart beating a mile a minute.

She had to find Henri. She had to tell him what she'd seen. They needed to discover what Steve was up to and prevent Yves, or someone else, from being murdered.

A shiver ran up her spine as she contemplated who that someone else might be. Given everything she had seen, she suspected that she might be high up on the list of possible victims.

Before she could move, the kitchen door swung open and Kris appeared. Through the open door, Ava could see Max basting a leg of lamb. Next to him, Lili was placing chocolate-covered profiteroles on a serving plate. The small cream-filled pastry puffs were one of Ava's favorite desserts.

"We eat early at the abbey. Dinner is in thirty minutes," Kris announced curtly. "Please be prompt."

Remembering that Kris was a true believer, Ava decided to play her role of a "chosen one" to the hilt. In a humble, awe-struck tone, she spoke, "I'm grateful to be here. Yves said it was a special place. He was right. In the abbey, I was overwhelmed by a deep sense of spirituality. I've never felt anything like that. The work is going to change my life."

Kris's steely glance was grudgingly replaced with a smile and a warmer tone of voice. "The work is life-changing. Maybe your coming here was ordained..."

"Is the work linked to the abbey?" Ava asked.

Kris laughed. "Everything has a lodestone. The abbey is the work's lodestone. The work draws energy from the abbey, and the abbey draws energy from the work. Without each other, they would be lost. Don't forget. Dinner in thirty minutes in the dining room."

"Where is the library? Bea said I could choose a book to read. I have trouble sleeping in new places," Ava said sheepishly.

"You won't have trouble sleeping here. It's very peaceful," Kris replied. "If you do want a book, the library is down that hallway, then cross the courtyard into the old annex. The annex was built at the same time as the abbey. It's all that's left of the original building."

"Thank you," Ava said. She watched Kris walk off. As soon as she was out of sight, Ava broke into a trot. At the end of the hallway, she opened the door, stepped into the courtyard and ran straight into Bea.

"Is the library there?" Ava asked, pointing at the old

annex.

"Yes," Bea responded. "Fiction is on the ground floor if you're looking for something light to read. You haven't seen Luc, have you?"

"No, sorry," Ava replied.

Bea entered the manor house. Ava continued through the courtyard to the library. Halfway there, she froze.

A black motorcycle was leaning against an ivy-covered wall. Stunned, she hurried over to it.

Could this be the motorcycle that tried to run Yves over?

She examined it carefully, comparing it with what she remembered.

It was the right size.

It was black.

There was mud on its license plate.

That didn't mean that it was the same motorcycle.

Ava felt a presence behind her. She turned. A frowning Max was standing there.

"I was looking at the bike," Ava said. "It's vintage, isn't it?"

"Vintage?" Max burst out laughing. "It's been here as long as I have. I suppose it is vintage. It belonged to the abbey's late owner. Do you ride?" he asked, studying Ava's face as she responded.

"It's on my bucket list of things to do," Ava said. "It's a shame no one uses it."

"People use it when they need to. It's the fastest way to get to town," Max said. "Do you know Yves well?"

"Not at all... I only met him once. He made a huge impression on me. I've never encountered anyone so special."

A strange look appeared on Max's face. "Yves is unique."

Ava didn't know if that was good or bad. She decided it was time to end the conversation. "I'll see you at dinner," she said and hotfooted it to the library, her mind on overdrive.

Could Max be the person who tried to run Yves over?

If not, who was he referring to when he said "people" used the motorcycle when they needed it? Ava had thought of asking him. That would have been like hanging a "sleuth" sign over her head, if Max was the one who had tried to run Yves over.

Without looking back, Ava entered the library. The moment she stepped inside she was overwhelmed by the heady scent of old books. The scent was a mix of leather bindings, old paper and heavy printing ink. It was an intoxicating scent to any old book lover.

The library was a large room with a wooden mezzanine that ran all the way around it.

Bookshelves lined its walls.

Modern overhead track lighting lit the room.

Cozy armchairs with colorful embroidered cushions were scattered around. Floor lamps stood next to them. Each chair had its own footstool.

If she weren't trying to find a killer, Ava would have grabbed a book and settled into one of the chairs, reading to her heart's delight.

But she had a would-be killer to find.

Ava looked around for Henri. Puzzled, she didn't see any sign of him.

Could he have left?

Hearing a noise, she jumped.

"Henri?"

"I'm up here," Henri shouted down from the mezzanine.

Ava stepped sideways and tilted her head back. Henri was standing in the far corner of the mezzanine at the top of a tall wooden ladder that ran to the ceiling. He was examining the books on the top shelves.

"Come down from there. You're making me dizzy."

Henri climbed down the ladder. He then clambered down the narrow stairway. He strode over to Ava who was sitting on the edge of an armchair.

"Did you speak with Luc?"

Henri shook his head. "No. He wasn't here when Bea and I arrived. He'll be back."

"Why do you say that?"

Henri held up a pair of reading glasses.

Suddenly, they heard footsteps coming across the stone

courtyard. Henri glanced around the room. His eyes stopped on a high-backed Queen Anne wingchair. "Quick. Take a book and go sit there."

"What if Luc sees me?"

"Curl your feet up and he won't," Henri said.

Ava grabbed a book off a table and dashed to the chair. She sat down, curling her feet up under her and opened the book. Her heart was beating so loudly that she was sure Luc would hear it.

Luc entered the room and eyed Henri from head to foot. Before he could speak, Henri held up Luc's glasses.

"Is this what you've come for?"

"I can see you weren't fooled," Luc replied with a laugh. "I did leave them deliberately. I wanted to speak to you without Bea. What are you doing here?"

"My job. I'm an expert in antiquarian books."

Luc raised his eyebrows. "What happened to the famous notary?"

"He retired."

"Don't worry. I didn't tell Bea who you were. It would only worry her more," Luc said with a heavy sigh.

Henri watched Luc, silent.

Luc hesitated. He then began to speak. "Until you appeared yesterday, Bea thought Yves was dead. I told her he was as alive as could be. Yves Dubois has no intention of leaving this earth. She wouldn't believe me."

"And now she does?"

"She believes you. Besides, dead men don't write letters. I'm sure Bea told you, if you hadn't figured it out by now, that I want to marry her. I've wanted that ever since the university."

"Why didn't you marry her then?"

"You haven't met Yves," Luc said. It was a statement not a question.

"No, I haven't," Henri responded.

"Yves is not only handsome, he is charm itself. If I had to choose between Yves and me twenty years ago, I'd have chosen him, too. Even then, he was a star."

"And now?"

"Yves is my friend. If I thought there was a chance for them, I wouldn't interfere. But since Yves inherited the abbey, he's changed and not for the better. He's become the great Yves Dubois. Bea intends to ask him for a divorce. I want to ask his permission to marry her."

Henri was startled. "Why do you need his permission?"

"That way, he can remain in our lives. Bea may want to leave him, but she doesn't want to lose him. Does that make any sense?"

"On the contrary, it makes total sense," Henri replied. "Yves must be exceptional."

"He is. With exceptional qualities and exceptional faults...

How did you get involved with him?"

"As I said, I've never met him. I received a letter to look at his books, and I accepted."

"Who is Mr. Sext, the other man in the letter?"

"A good friend I worked with until his death last year. He was also an expert in antiquarian books."

"Maybe Yves knew him?"

"Perhaps," Henri said.

Luc eyed Henri. "You may be here as a book appraiser, but I have no doubt that you've checked up on Yves Dubois."

"To find out what?"

"I won't play cat and mouse with you. Yves borrowed money for the abbey. Bea let him use her apartment as collateral. Now he has to pay the loan back."

Henri's expression remained neutral. "Can he?"

"I don't know. The regional government wants to buy the abbey and its land. He refused. Before he went to Italy, he told her that he'd found a solution and that she shouldn't worry."

"And since then?"

"She's worried," Luc said. "Bea's invited us for a drink in the sitting room before dinner. We should go."

Seated in the high-backed wingchair, Ava waited until the voices had drifted off before standing up. She shook her legs to get the blood flowing. As she waited, she thought of what Luc had said: Yves had found a way to get the money before his trip to Italy.

Was the money the reason someone was trying to kill him?

Ava left the library. When she stepped into the courtyard, she noticed that the motorcycle was gone. She hurried to the manor house. Entering, she ran straight into Kris.

Kris smiled at her. "Did you find a book?"

Ava looked down at her empty hands. "There were so many to choose from that I thought I'd leave it for later."

A frowning Kris watched her leave.

CHAPTER 16

"Being chosen means you're a special person. You have a special link to the universe. That link means you must ensure the continuation of the work. The work is your life," Kris said with passion as she stood at the head of the table. Her eyes moved from person to person, as if she were addressing each one individually. "Your life is the work. Nothing is more important. The work is more important than life itself."

As Kris continued to speak, Ava glanced around the dining room table to gauge the reactions of the others. Steve was running his finger absently around the rim of his wine glass, his mind elsewhere. Margot kept glancing over her shoulder at the dining room door. Arnaud's eyes were fixed on Lili who was becoming more and more agitated with each of Kris's words. Only Max was really listening to Kris's speech and he did so with the utmost attention. In fact, his eyes were glued to her in admiration.

Was his reaction a sign of fervent belief in the work or something else? Ava wondered as she shifted in her chair, trying unsuccessfully to focus on what Kris was saying.

After meeting a dead man who wasn't dead, being chosen by the universe as a special person and surviving a dunk in the Canal St. Martin on a warm spring evening that might or might not have been an attempted murder, listening to a series of dull spiritual speeches by members of the inner circle was a serious let down.

First, Max had spoken. He was a poor speaker. His speech was vague and full of platitudes on believing in yourself and your fellow man. Strangely, he never mentioned Yves or the work.

This was followed by an extremely long speech by Margot. While she did mention Yves, she then spoke about everything under the sun except how the chosen ones became masters of the universe, a subject that Ava found fascinating now that she was a chosen one.

On the other hand, if she really were on the path to becoming a master of the universe, she probably wouldn't have needed a flyer to discover this. It would be clear to everyone. There would be a neon sign blinking on and off over her head that said: *Ava Sext, Master of the Universe...*

If angels had wings, then why couldn't a master of the

universe have a neon sign blinking on and off over his head?

Ava had no idea how that could possibly come about, but then she wasn't a master of the universe, yet.

With a sigh, she imagined that the real chosen ones were probably lolling about on their own private islands in the South Pacific or meditating on mountaintops in the Himalayas, enjoying the fruits of their lofty position.

Speaking of fruits, a starved Ava looked around the table for something to eat. A breadbasket full of crispy French country bread that made her mouth water was on the other side of the table. To reach it, she would have to stand up and lean over the table to grab it. She refrained, certain that doing so might affect her position as a novice chosen one.

Kris was now droning on about how the universe was there for us when we least expect it.

Ava glanced enviously at Henri, Bea and Luc who were in the adjoining sitting room. Having been spared the agony of listening to the speeches, they were chatting over a glass of wine and some wild boar sausage. Ava wished she could join them. She was sure that she would be able to glean something from speaking with Bea and Luc. Not that Ava doubted Henri's information gathering skills... Far from it.

It was just that Henri was French.

In fact, Henri was the essence of Frenchness. His former position as a French notary meant he knew how to read between the lines and understand France's secret cultural codes that were invisible to foreigners. However, as a foreigner, Ava was sure she'd see things that were invisible to the French.

Turning her attention back to the table, Ava took note of the two people who were missing: the young man with the flyers and Yves, although his presence hung heavy in the room.

Ava eyed everyone at the table. *Could the killer be among them?*

She was astonished at how cold-blooded she had become. She didn't find the idea of a killer lurking nearby the least bit disturbing. However, she immediately regretted choosing the term "*cold-blooded*" to describe her state of mind. The less she saw of blood the better.

Loud applause broke out.

Ava glanced up. Kris had finished her speech and had sat down. Max and Arnaud were applauding enthusiastically. A cutting glance from Kris put an end to their applause.

Kris rose to her feet again and tapped her wine glass with a spoon. Thinking this meant that dinner would be served, Ava wanted to shout "hallelujah" until she heard the fatal words that participants in any group event hate to hear.

"While Max and Margot make the last minute preparations for dinner, I'll ask our two newcomers to introduce themselves."

As Max and Margot headed to the kitchen, Kris beamed at

Steve and Ava.

"Who would like to go first?"

Judging from Steve's uncomfortable look, Ava was not alone is her aversion to this exercise in self-revelation.

Seizing the floor, Ava smiled at Kris and Steve. "I'll let Steve go first as he's come all the way from California to be with us tonight."

Steve gave her a withering look. However, he smiled graciously and began to speak. "I'm not a chosen one. I'm just interested in the work. Yves spoke to me at length about it. I'm especially interested in his discoveries on eternal life."

Lili and Arnaud looked at each other, puzzled.

"I don't understand," Lili said with a frown.

"Yves told me that he had found the secret to eternal life."

Shaken, Kris spoke. "He shouldn't have told you that. That's only for the inner circle."

"I didn't know anything about it, and I was close to Yves," Lili protested, glaring at Kris in open hostility.

"There are different ways of being close to him," Kris said dismissively. "Yves didn't share secrets with just anyone."

Bursting into tears, Lili jumped up. Arnaud grabbed her arm and pulled her down, whispering in her ear.

Ava frowned.

Eternal life?

That was what Bea must have meant in the abbey when

she said that Yves had found a way to beat death.

Unaware of what was happening, Max carried a platter of sliced lamb and roast potatoes into the room.

"The lamb is cooked to perfection," he said, placing the platter in the center of the table. Margot followed him in with a large bowl of salad greens. She was astonished to see the tears on Lili's face.

"Are you OK, Lili?"

Arnaud answered for Lili. "She'll be fine," he said with a glance at Kris.

Margot turned and eyed Kris. Ignoring the tension, Kris took two decanters of wine off a serving cart and set them on the table. She walked to the sitting room.

"Dinner," Kris said to Bea, Luc and Henri.

Content that she had escaped having to introduce herself in the blowback from Steve's comments, Ava wondered why Kris had been upset about his revealing Yves's discoveries on eternal life.

To Ava, finding the key to eternal life sounded like something you read about in a sci-fi novel, too impossible to be true. She eyed Steve. Why would he be interested in it? He wasn't even thirty. Eternal life seemed like something you turned your attention to as you got older.

As Bea, Henri and Luc walked into the dining room and took their seats, Margot eyed the door.

"When did Yves say he was coming?" she asked Kris.

"He didn't say. I assume he'll be here this weekend," Kris responded evasively.

"Are we even sure that he's alive?" Lili asked.

With a glance at Henri, Bea answered her in a tone that brooked no dissent. "You're being ridiculous. I can assure you that Yves is very much alive. As for his whereabouts, my husband will appear when it suits him, and only he knows when that is."

With a less hostile look than usual, Kris nodded at Bea. "I couldn't agree more. I suggest we eat."

In response, Margot sat down. Max served everyone. When he handed Lili her plate, she stood up, pale-faced.

"Excuse me, I'm not hungry," she said and left the room.

"Lili, wait!" Arnaud shouted. "Excuse me," he said. He jumped up and ran out after her.

Ava frowned. At the Canal St. Martin, Lili had been sure that Yves was dead, and that Arnaud knew about it.

Could that mean that Arnaud was involved in Yves's disappearance?

Ava added Arnaud to her list of suspects, a list that kept getting longer and longer. If this kept up, she and Henri would soon be on it.

As Max finished serving, he sat down and looked around the dining room. "I want to thank the work for keeping me at the abbey. It's changed my life. As much as I admire Yves, the work is much bigger than one man."

Ava studied Max's face. The more she saw him, the more she was sure he was a familiar stranger. She wished she could pinpoint where she had seen him.

"Tell us about the gardens, Max," Bea said, artfully changing the subject. She turned to the others. "Max is the one who created the magical gardens that surround the house. They're the only things that make the manor house worth coming to."

"Not everyone has the spiritual depth to appreciate the abbey," Kris said.

"Please spare me. I'm glad I lack the necessary depth," Bea responded.

Before Kris could say anything more, Max began to speak about the gardens and how they'd changed over the last twenty years.

Ava guessed that Max was in his forties. That meant he had spent almost most of his adult life here. She wondered how long Kris had been coming to the abbey.

As Ava ate the wonderful dinner – lamb, perfectly cooked with just the right touch of wild garlic and rosemary, and oven potatoes that melted in your mouth -- she had a hard time keeping her mind on the upcoming murder. Ava took a sip of the light red wine from the Loire Valley. It went perfectly with the lamb. She felt guilty that epicurean pleasures were cutting into her sleuthing. However, even detectives had to eat.

Hadn't many of Agatha Christie's books had table scenes?

Of course, a number of those dinners had ended up with someone being poisoned, Ava thought as she helped herself to more lamb.

Kris was silent throughout dinner. Steve appeared unaffected by the tension at the table, although he ate like a bird. Ava wondered if that was because he wasn't hungry or if eternal life required a special diet. Margot remained silent while Henri ate with real enthusiasm.

"The meal is superb. Bravo to the chef," Henri said with an appreciative nod.

"Max is a wonderful cook. He should open a restaurant rather than staying holed up here," Bea added.

"My cooking is a reflection of the abbey. If I left, I'd probably never cook again," Max said.

"Are you a book lover, Henri?" Kris asked.

Henri grinned. "More than that. Books are my life. I'm here to appraise Yves's collection."

Kris was shocked. "Yves is selling his books?"

"Does Yves know you're here?" Max asked.

"Yves was the one who invited Henri. Luc and I are only here to keep him company," Bea said.

Kris looked at Max oddly.

Taking this as his cue, Max rose. "While Margot and I clear

the table, why don't the rest of you move into sitting room."

When the others stood and moved toward the sitting room, Ava grabbed some plates. Steve also pitched in to helped clear the table.

The tension in the kitchen was so thick you could cut it with a knife. Max kept glancing toward the sitting room while Margot tidied the kitchen.

When Max started to put coffee cups on a cart, Ava turned to Margot who was now scrolling through a cell phone she had picked up off the counter.

"Is there anything I can do to help?" Ava asked.

Startled, Margot looked up from the phone. "No. Everything is under control. Thanks."

Ava glanced around the kitchen one last time and headed to the sitting room. When she got there, Henri and Bea were chatting. Kris was standing alone at the far end of the room, brooding.

If this were a film, the murderer would strike now, Ava thought.

Instead of a killer with a gun, Margot stormed into the room with the cell phone in her hand. Shaking with anger, she headed directly to Kris. She pulled her aside and spoke to her in a loud whisper. Ava was close enough to hear what they were saying.

"Did you really speak to Yves yesterday evening?" Margot whispered.

"Of course I did," Kris said. She grabbed Margot's arm and pulled her into the dining room.

Ava inched toward them.

"How?" Margot insisted.

"Yves called me on my cell phone," Kris said quickly.

Margot waved the cell phone in the air. "You're lying. I just checked. There were no calls from Yves yesterday. In fact, there were no calls at all for the entire time we were at the lecture. Why did you lie?"

Kris's face went red. "I won't permit you to…"

Max strode into the dining room. He stopped when he saw Kris's expression. "What's going on?"

"In Italy, Yves said he was unhappy with the direction the two of you wanted to take the work in. I didn't believe him," Margot said.

"Ask Margot what happened when Yves told her he wanted to stop seeing her," Kris said to Max.

Margot's face turned bright red. "Kris, I don't know what game you're playing, but you're going to regret it." She spun around and left.

Max grabbed Kris by the arm. "Did you talk with Yves or not?" Max asked.

In response, Kris stormed off. Max stood there with an odd look on his face. When he noticed Ava staring at him, he left.

Ava's mind was racing. She wasn't surprised that Kris had lied about speaking with Yves. She had guessed that. But now she also knew that Max and Kris were trying to take over the work and that Yves had been seeing Lili and Margot! It was just like Henri had said... love and money!

Ava walked back into the sitting room.

"Where is everyone?" Bea asked, frowning. Without waiting for an answer, she continued, "The light show starts in forty-five minutes. I suggest we have coffee afterwards. Maybe by then everyone will have calmed down." She rose to her feet and left.

Ava dashed over to Henri. "Something's going to happen! I can feel it." Ava whispered. "It's like a storm about to break."

Before she could tell him what she had heard in the dining room, a loud shout came from the courtyard.

It was followed by another loud shout.

"That's Steve!" Henri said as he dashed off.

Ava ran after him, hoping that her premonition about someone getting murdered was wrong.

CHAPTER 17

Luc was sprawled on the floor of the library's upper mezzanine. His eyes were closed. His breathing troubled. Panicked, Steve was standing over him.

"Will he be OK?" Steve asked Henri who was kneeling next to Luc.

"His pulse is strong," Henri said as he propped Luc's head up.

Groggy, Luc opened his eyes. He blinked several times when he saw Henri, Steve and Ava staring at him. "What's with the gloomy expressions?" he joked as he tried to lift his head. "Ouch," he said, grimacing.

Bea and Max came running into the library. Bea dashed up the stairs to the mezzanine and pushed Henri and Steve aside. She crouched down next to Luc and took his hand in hers.

"What happened, darling?" Bea asked.

Luc looked around to get his bearings. "I went up the

ladder to look for a book I'd seen earlier. The lights went out. I heard a noise below. I turned and fell. It was stupid on my part."

Henri looked worried. "The lights were off when we got here."

"They were on when I went up the stairs," Luc said.

"Did someone attack you?" Bea asked. "Tell me the truth."

Luc smiled wanly. "Nothing so dramatic. I was just surprised when the lights went out. I heard a noise and fell."

Bea stared into Luc's eyes. "You're sure you didn't see anyone?"

"The Ghost of Christmas Past could have been standing next to me, and I wouldn't have seen him. It was pitch black, Bea," Luc said as he smiled at her, still holding her hand.

Max stepped forward. "There's a problem with the electrical current in the annex. That might account for the lights going off."

"Or maybe someone did it deliberately," Bea said as she helped Luc up. "I'll drive you to the hospital."

Luc's expression darkened. "No doctors. I'm fine. I just need to rest."

"Max, help me get him to Yves's quarters. I can watch him better that way."

Max helped Luc to his feet. Leaning on Bea and Max, a limping Luc started to the stairs.

"Luc, what book were you looking for?" Henri asked.

"Just a history book," Luc replied vaguely.

Henri smiled. "Do you want me to bring it to you?"

"I don't even remember what it's called. I'd know it if I saw it. It's there somewhere," Luc said waving his hand at the thousands of books on the bookshelves. "I just don't remember where."

They all went down to the ground floor.

When the others left the library leaving Ava and Henri alone, Ava turned to him. "What really happened?"

"Luc fell. That's all we know for sure," Henri replied as he walked over to an armchair and sat down, plumping the pillow behind his back. He pointed to the mezzanine. "The lights were out when I arrived, but when I hit the switch they went on. They had been turned off. So it wasn't a problem of electricity. Luc's lucky he didn't topple over the banister."

Ava narrowed her eyes, deep in thought. "He said something startled him. Was it something or someone?"

"My guess is someone. Bea believes it was Yves."

Ava's face showed her astonishment. "How do you know that?"

"From her reaction. She asked Luc several times if he had seen someone."

Puzzled, Ava shook her head. "Why would Yves try and hurt Luc?"

"Maybe Yves only wanted to speak to Luc. Or maybe it wasn't Yves at all. Luc said he didn't see anyone."

"He might be lying," Ava said.

"That's a possibility," Henri said with a frown.

"What's your theory?"

"I have no idea what happened here, but something is going on. Something serious. The bridge was sabotaged."

Ava reeled back in shock. "Max said it was the rain and a lack of repair."

Henri shook his head. "I examined it carefully. Someone had loosened the boards."

"To frighten you?" Ava asked, trying to integrate the new information into what she already knew.

"The water wasn't deep enough for us to drown. The bridge was a warning to someone. I don't know if it was meant for us."

"Like my dunk in the canal," Ava said. "That means someone is running around leaving warnings…"

"While someone else is getting ready to strike," Henri said.

Both fell silent.

"There's something else. Margot checked Kris's phone. There were no calls from Yves or anyone else yesterday evening. I also learned that Margot was seeing Yves."

Henri's expression didn't change.

"You're not surprised?" Ava asked.

"We both suspected that the call was a lie. As for Yves having a relationship with Margot... that doesn't surprise me at all. It would surprise me more if he wasn't having a relationship with her."

Ava frowned. She guessed that this was a case where Henri's knowledge of French men was more extensive than hers. She wondered how Yves had time to promote the work with all the women he was seeing.

"Did Margot say anything else?" Henri asked.

"Yes. Yves believed that Kris and Max were trying to hijack the work." Ava took a deep breath. "Why would Kris lie? What's the point?"

Henri leaned forward and drummed his fingers on his knee. "A lot of reasons. Maybe she believes Yves is dead. It might be a power grab."

Ava's face lit up. "I almost forgot Steve... He came to the abbey after you and Bea left. He waited for someone outside its walls for about ten minutes. When the person didn't arrive, he left."

"The same Steve who said he was too tired to come to the abbey with us?" Henri asked.

Ava nodded. "The man with the flyers is here. I saw him in the garden earlier. When I ran out to see if I could catch him, Steve was there and the man was gone."

"For someone who just arrived in France, Steve seems to

be everywhere. You're sure he didn't meet anyone at the abbey."

"I'm sure. I waited until he left. I followed him at a distance. When he headed to the front door, I went through the garden to the back door. I heard someone in the bushes. I called out to them, but they ran off."

Henri was silent. He knitted his brow, deep in thought.

"On the ride here, Steve was astonished to learn that Yves had disappeared. He appeared worried until he learned when it had happened."

Henri caught the gist of her thoughts. "So Yves invited Steve to the abbey after his disappearance."

"Yes."

"Then Steve is here for a reason beyond the work. My bet is eternal life."

"He's not even thirty. Why would he care about eternal life?" Ava asked.

"I agree it doesn't make sense, but that's all we have to go on," Henri said.

"Did you learn anything on the drive down?" Ava asked.

"Only what Bea said in the abbey. She's fed up with the work, the abbey and the chosen ones. She wants to move on."

"Is that good or bad?"

Henri raised his eyebrows and shrugged his shoulders. "Hard to say."

"Henri, you were a notary. It's the type of situation you probably encountered thousands of times."

Henri burst out laughing. "Contrary to your vivid imagination, not all French people go around murdering others for love and money."

"But some do," Ava insisted.

"Some do," Henri acknowledged.

"Did Yves cancel the seminar or was it someone impersonating him who did it?"

"We'll have to ask Yves," Henri replied.

"He's here?" Ava asked. Immediately, her heart began to beat faster at the thought of meeting her tall dark-haired stranger again.

"I believe so," Henri said rising to his feet. "It was a mistake for Bea to announce that she intended to sell the abbey."

"Why?"

"With everything that's going on, it's wise to add fuel to the fire."

Suddenly, a thought hit Ava. "Maybe the person who frightened Luc intended to kill him. Steve's arrival prevented him from completing his task."

"That's possible," Henri said.

"I've come to like Yves. I'd be disappointed if he turned out to be a killer," Ava said.

Henri chuckled. "Now you sound like your Uncle Charles. He would have forgiven the devil himself."

"I almost forgot. I saw a black motorcycle in the courtyard."

"The same one?" Henri asked as his eyes lit up.

"I have no idea. To me, all black motorcycles look alike. When I was examining it, Max appeared. He said that everyone in the abbey used it.

Henri eyed Ava. "Was Max disturbed that you'd seen it?"

"No."

"That could mean two things... He wasn't the one who tried to run Yves over or he was the one and didn't recognize you."

Ava frowned. "There's a third possibility. He was the one who tried to run Yves over, and he did recognize me."

Henri didn't say anything. His silence spoke louder than words, and Ava didn't like what she was hearing.

"What are we going to do now?" Ava asked.

"I'm going to talk with Luc alone and find out what really happened. He might tell me things he wouldn't tell Bea."

"Such as?" Ava asked.

"I have no idea. That's why I need to see him."

Ava gritted her teeth. She was sure that Henri had a special reason for seeing Luc, a reason he had no intention of sharing with her. "Do you know who's leaving the warnings?"

"Of course," Henri said.

Ava's eyes widened. "You do? Who?"

"The butler. Isn't that what happens in all British mysteries?" Henri teased.

"While you're speaking with Luc, I'm going to see what the others are up to," Ava said, not amused by Henri's French humor.

As they walked to the library door, he turned to her, deadly serious. "Ava, no matter what happens, don't go to the abbey alone. Promise me."

Ava didn't say anything.

Henri stared at her, waiting for her to answer.

"I promise," Ava said as she crossed her fingers behind her back.

CHAPTER 18

Leaving the library, Ava wandered through the ground floor of the manor house. The kitchen was empty. The dining room was also empty, and no one was in the sitting room. So much for her plan to see what the others were doing. Taking the stairs two at a time, Ava dashed upstairs.

The idea that Yves might have tried to kill Luc in the library or frighten him disturbed her. She wanted to save an innocent man from being murdered. She had no desire to save the life of a man who went around trying to kill people when they weren't trying to kill him.

But then life was complicated and being a detective was even more complicated.

Ava was sure her that late uncle would have had a lot to say on the matter.

When she reached the upper hallway, she slowed and listened. Everything was quiet. If people were up to something, they were doing it silently.

She crossed the hallway and entered her room. The second she set foot inside, she knew someone had been there. She could feel it. Nothing looked out of order, but her senses shouted that someone had been there. She eyed her clothing on the bench at the end of the bed. It was folded exactly as she had left it, yet somehow it looked different.

She went into the bathroom. Someone had also been there. Frowning, she studied the beauty products on the glass shelf next to the sink. What could her pear-scented face wash, orange blossom cream and cinnamon-flavored toothpaste reveal to an intruder other than she smelled like a fruit salad?

She made a mental note to harmonize her beauty products for her next sleuthing adventure.

Stepping back into the bedroom, she surveyed the room. She checked the luggage tag on her overnight bag. It still had her old London address on it.

Her heart beating, she walked over to the armchair where she had hidden her notebook. The cushions didn't look like they had been moved. She picked up the seat cushion. Her notebook was there. It was then she noticed a pen on the floor next to the chair: the pen that had been inside her notebook.

Someone had read her notes.

Ava sank to the ground in despair.

Someone at the manor house now knew that she was

investigating Yves's disappearance. Paging through her notebook, she saw that her notes were short and cryptic. There was no mention of Henri. She thanked her lucky stars that her handwriting was so illegible. Whoever had found her notebook would have had trouble reading it.

Still, this was a self-induced error she could have done without. She put the notebook back under the cushion. If someone had read it, she didn't want them to know that she was on to them, whoever they were.

She walked over to the window and eyed the garden. It was completely dark. The tall trees that lined it meant that darkness fell earlier there. This time, there was no sign of Steve or the young man. No one appeared to be lurking in the bushes.

Ava headed back into the hallway. When she went by Lili's room, she heard Lili and Arnaud arguing.

After checking that she was alone, Ava moved towards the closed door. Behind it, she could hear Lili speaking:

"Yves isn't coming. There's no point in waiting for him."

Arnaud let out a loud sigh. "I'm sick of this. Yves will appear when he wants to appear."

Lili sobbed. "He isn't coming, and Kris didn't speak with him…"

"How do you know that?"

"Because Yves is dead."

Arnaud's tone changed. He was now almost whispering. "Lili, I won't tell anyone what I saw on the mountain. I promise."

Ava pressed her ear against the door to catch what he was saying.

"What you saw? What did you see?" Lili asked in a puzzled, aggressive tone.

"I saw you go up the mountain," Arnaud said.

"Why were you following me?"

"I love you. I want to protect you. Yves is a ladies' man who moves from woman to woman."

"I'm different. We're going to live together," Lili protested.

"Live together? He has a wife!" Arnaud said with a snort.

"He's going to divorce her."

"Lili... They've been married twenty years. That's what men always say."

"Yves is not any man. He means what he says," Lili replied. "No, Yves is dead. If he were alive, he would have called me. Someone killed him."

"Lili, I promise I won't tell anyone what you did."

"What I did..." Lili said, raising her voice. "What did I do?"

Outside in the hallway, Ava froze. The idea that Lili had tried to kill Yves had never occurred to her.

"When you didn't come back down the mountain, I went

up to see what was going on. I intended to speak with Yves, man to man."

"How dare you interfere in my life," Lili said angrily. "What did you say to him?"

"Nothing. I couldn't. When I reached the lookout point, he was lying on the ground, unconscious. I left."

"You left him lying there?" Lili said in outrage and horror.

"I wanted him to suffer. If he were out of the picture, it would be better for us."

"What did you do with his body?" Lili asked.

"Body? Nothing. Halfway down the mountain, I turned around and went back to help him."

Ava could hear Lili crying.

"When I reached the lookout point, he was gone," Arnaud said.

"Gone? Where did he go?" Lili asked, alarmed.

"He must have regained consciousness and left by the back path."

"Or maybe someone dragged his body to the edge of the cliff and tossed it into the Mediterranean!"

"Who would have done that?" Arnaud asked.

"The person who attacked him," Lili said.

"You attacked him," Arnaud replied, his voice sputtering.

"Why would I do that? I love Yves. If he's dead, it's all your fault. If you'd helped him, he'd still be alive."

"Yves isn't dead, Lili. Dead men don't make phone calls. He spoke with Kris."

"If Yves was alive, he would have contacted me," Lili insisted, weeping.

"Lili, stop. You know what this means?"

"What?" Lili asked.

"If you didn't knock him out, someone else did. That person might be here."

"Who could it be?" Lili asked.

"It could be anyone. Max, Margot, Kris… One of the others might even have been in Italy," Arnaud said.

"Or it could have been you, Arnaud. It could have been you," Lili said coldly.

In the hallway, Ava's mind went into overdrive. *Who helped Yves get away? Did he escape on his own?*

If Yves had been attacked and Lili and Arnaud didn't do it, that left Kris, Margot and Max… Or it could have been Bea, Luc or Steve.

The murderer was always the last one you suspected in detective novels. But as Ava suspected everyone, that theory didn't help her at all.

She was frustrated. She wished her Uncle Charles had written a manual. His "turn it upside down" rule meant that everyone at the manor house could be a murderer… even her.

Afraid Lili and Arnaud would discover her eavesdropping,

Ava hurried down the steps to the ground floor. She needed to speak to Henri A.S.A.P. She halted at the bottom of the stairs when she remembered that she and Henri didn't know one another. She certainly couldn't ask to have a private word with him.

CHAPTER 19

When Ava reached the sitting room, it was empty. Frustrated, she settled into a corner armchair to wait for the others.

Arnaud was right. The would-be murder was at the manor house or on the grounds.

Hell's bells!

From what she had learned since she had arrived at the manor house, everyone seemed to be intent on killing someone else.

Was Arnaud a murderer?

Maybe Lili was unhinged and had tried to kill Yves but didn't remember it.

Ava paused.

Anyone who had the phrase "hell's bells" running through their mind was under severe stress.

Shifting in her chair, a new angle occurred to her.

Someone had attacked Yves. He didn't see who did it. He cancelled the seminar, inviting only those he felt might have done it. The letter to Sext and DeAth was so he'd have a crime-busting backup team to help him root out his would-be killer.

Hearing voices, Ava looked up.

"I'm fine, Bea. You're making a mountain out of a molehill. No one tried to hurt me. I heard a noise. I was startled. I fell. No bones broken," Luc protested as he entered the sitting room leaning on Bea's arm.

"You shouldn't have gotten up," Bea said in a protective tone as she helped him into a chair by the door.

From her seat, Ava noted that Bea was no longer hiding her feelings for Luc as she had earlier. On the contrary, Luc's fall appeared to have cemented Bea's feelings for him and forced her to choose between Luc and Yves. Of course, this was just Ava's layperson view of the situation. Maybe if Yves were to suddenly appear, Bea would fall under his charm again. But given the way Bea was acting toward Luc, Ava doubted it.

Henri strode into the room. He headed directly toward Bea and Luc. "I'm looking forward to seeing the famous light show."

"It's magical," Bea said with real enthusiasm. "Yves created an illusion that is truer than life. I doubt a rebuilt abbey would have the same effect."

"We'll never know that," Kris said curtly as she entered the room.

"I'm glad we won't. Otherwise Yves would be broke," Bea said, unperturbed by Kris's snappy tone.

Henri glanced over at Ava.

His eyes seemed to be saying: *In France, the motive is usually love, money... or both.*

Ava wished she had some way of signaling him that they needed to talk. But as they hadn't set up a secret code between them, she could only mull over the love and money angle again.

If it was money, Bea had a motive. Since Luc intended to marry her, Bea's money issues would become his. Therefore, Luc also had a motive. Max and Kris might also be plotting to get their hands on the abbey. After all, Max had spent much of his life here.

If it was love, from what Ava had learned so far, the manor house was a battleground with wounded hearts piling up, knee-deep... To begin with, Bea was married to Yves and still had feelings for him. Lili was madly in love with Yves and believed they would one day live together. Margot appeared to have been seeing him, too. For all Ava knew, Kris might secretly be in love with Yves. Jealousy was a possible motive for Arnaud and Luc.

The only person who didn't seem to fall into either category was Steve. Ava guessed that he had come for the secret of eternal life.

Maybe the abbey had a fountain of youth or some secret herb that bestowed eternal life hidden on its premises...

The Yves that Ava had met two days earlier was a handsome man. However, he didn't look especially young. If she were to learn that he really was ninety that would be something. But since he had been at the university with Luc and Bea that was not the case.

She turned her thoughts back to Steve. Maybe he was doing research on the subject of eternal life.

Just then, Steve entered the room. Ava examined him closely. With a slight leap of imagination, she could see him in a laboratory working late into the night, stopping only to retape his glasses.

An odd rattling sound pulled her back to the present. Turning, she saw a smiling Margot wheel in a cart with cups and saucers on it.

"We've prepared everything for coffee now. That way, we can have it after the show. All we have to do is turn the coffee on."

Ava felt eyes on her. Looking up, she saw that Kris was staring at her, hostile. Fortunately for Ava, Max entered the room carrying a tray of profiteroles. He set it down on the coffee table.

"Those are Lili's famous desserts?" Ava asked. She rose to her feet and walked over to admire them. Despite the seriousness of the situation, she could feel her mouth watering. They looked delicious.

"What are they called again?" Steve asked, joining them.

"Profiteroles," Max replied.

Henri jumped into the conversation. "Making profiteroles is a real test for a pastry chef. You need to get the dough and the cream filling just right. The hardest part is putting it all together."

"They look mouth watering," Steve said. "Lili must be very talented."

Kris smiled oddly. "That's why she was chosen."

Ava glanced around the room. *Where were Lili and Arnaud?* If Lili had tried to murder Yves, she might have killed Arnaud when she learned that he knew about it.

As if on cue, a troubled Arnaud entered the room. "Has anyone seen Lili?"

Margot shook her head. "She's probably in the garden."

Without a word, Arnaud turned on his heels and left.

Ava was relieved that her latest theory was wrong and that Arnaud was alive.

Bea stood up, very lady of the house. "I suggest we go outside now. We want to be there before the light show starts. The best place to see it is directly in front of the abbey."

"How long does the show last?" Henri asked.

"It's on a timer," Max replied. "I set it for fifteen minutes.

Is that OK, Bea?"

That's perfect," Kris said before Bea could reply.

Ignoring Kris, Bea spoke to Max. "Fifteen minutes sounds fine."

Kris's face clouded over. The tension between the two women was so thick you could cut it with a knife. Clearly, Kris didn't accept Bea's intrusion into the manor house or the abbey.

Ava thought of Henri's theory again. The animosity between the two women sprang from which of them had the right to be the *chatelaine*, the woman in charge of the manor... Under Henri's theory, property was money. So money was at the heart of their dispute.

"Shall we go?" Bea asked. Without waiting for an answer, she headed to the door with Luc at her side. When Luc put his hand on her shoulder, Bea grasped it tenderly.

Chatting about French pastries, Henri and Steve followed them out.

Visibly angry, Kris hadn't moved since her verbal altercation with Bea.

Max strode over to her. "Let it go, Kris. Let it go."

Kris lit into him. "I'll decide whether I'll let it go or not. I don't need you telling me what to do."

After a nervous glance at Kris and Max, Margot walked over to Ava. "We should go outside. The light show will be starting."

Margot and Ava walked through the tall grass in the front garden. The grass was wet with dew. The night air was still warm, but it had an underlying chill to it that made Ava shiver. She pulled her jacket tightly around her shoulders. The star-filled sky and the full moon overhead lit the lawn so that it was bright enough to walk without a flashlight.

Margot eyed Ava. "You've come at a difficult time. People aren't usually like this. When Yves returns, he'll set things right."

"Have you heard from him?" Ava asked.

Margot's expression clouded over. She didn't answer Ava's question.

Up ahead, Ava could see Henri, Steve, Bea and Luc standing in front of the abbey. They were far enough back so they could see the entire facade when it lit up.

As Ava walked, she could hear Max and Kris behind her, whispering furiously. Their whispers were too soft for her to decipher what they were saying but loud enough to know they were arguing.

Bea turned when everyone arrived. "We were worried that you would miss the beginning. For me, the most beautiful moment is when the abbey goes from being a dark hull, cut out against the night sky, to becoming a living entity."

"The abbey doesn't need lights to be a living entity," Kris said. "Some of us can feel it."

Bea ignored her.

Arnaud hurried over to the group, distraught. "I can't find Lili."

Before anyone could answer, the abbey lit up. The lights gave the illusion that the ruins were an intact. The illusion was perfect. The abbey was magnificent.

Ava's breath was taken away.

Yves had managed to create an optical illusion that was not only powerful, but it also imbued the abbey with a mystical aura.

Henri walked over to Ava. "It's incredible, isn't it?"

"I'm in awe," Ava said, moved. Looking around, she could see that Margot was close enough to hear anything she might say to Henri. As much as she wanted to tell him about Lili and Arnaud, this was not the right time.

Margot walked over to Ava and Henri. "What do you think of the show?"

"It's very special," Henri said.

Ava nodded. "I've never seen anything like it."

"What did Yves tell you about the abbey?" Margot asked Henri.

Right away, Ava saw that Henri was on guard.

"Nothing. I've never met Yves, although I do hope to

meet him this weekend. From what people say, he's an exceptional person," Henri replied.

"He's more than that," Margot said in a sudden burst of fervor. "He's the one who makes the abbey and the work special."

"You were here before Yves inherited the abbey, weren't you?" Henri asked.

"We were a small group back then. Max was the first one. But then he'd spent years at the abbey before Gilbert, Yves's late uncle, discovered the work. Max is more involved with the abbey than the work."

"When did Gilbert discover the work?" Henri asked.

Margot frowned, trying to pinpoint the exact date. "About six years ago. He found an ancient manuscript that spoke about the chosen ones and the work. I heard Gilbert lecture on it in Paris. I was skeptical until I came here. The work made sense at the abbey. Once you embrace it, your whole life changes... I know mine has."

"What happened to the manuscript?" Ava asked, curious. "Do we get to see it as chosen ones?" The notion that she might see a secret manuscript that held the wisdom of the ages was intoxicating.

"I wish we did. None of us ever saw it, not even Max," Margot replied.

Henri knitted his brow as he tried to put the pieces

together. "How was Yves able to take over the work if he hadn't seen the manuscript?"

Margot was astonished by Henri's question. "Yves is a master. We others are only chosen ones. We have to strive to become masters of the universe. Yves and his uncle were masters from the beginning. I'm certain that Yves saw the manuscript. It's probably in his possession now. Gilbert must have entrusted it to him before his death."

Right away, Ava saw a new motive. Glancing at Henri, she could see that they were on the same wavelength. Love and money were powerful reasons to kill someone but possessing the key to becoming a master of the universe would be equally as powerful, if not more so.

I might even kill for it, Ava thought before reining her baser instincts in. She was there to save Yves's life, not to become a master of the universe.

"Is there also a manuscript on eternal life?" Henri asked casually.

Margot shook her head. "Not that I know of."

"If Yves were to leave, who would take over the work?" Henri asked.

Margot raised her hand to her neck as if fending off a blow. "The work is Yves. Without him, there would just be Kris, Max and three or four other people who aren't here tonight."

"And Lili?" Henri asked.

"I doubt that Lili would stay without Yves," Margot replied. The expression on her face made her inner thoughts clear.

Ava noted that Margot had not included herself in the people who would remain if Yves left. Nor had she mentioned Arnaud.

Suddenly, the lights went off. The abbey was dark. The group stood in complete blackness as dark clouds now obscured the full moon overhead.

Ava was puzzled. The abbey had only been lit up for five minutes, not fifteen.

"Max, what's going on?" Bea shouted out into the darkness.

"I don't know. I'll go check the generator," Max said as he lit a match and walked off toward the abbey.

"Let's go and have coffee," Bea said. "If Max gets the generator working, we can come back later."

Henri took out his phone and turned on its flashlight. "This will get us back to the manor house without breaking a leg."

Luc took a lighter out of his pocket, lit it and walked up to Henri. "Follow us," he said to the others.

Bea hurried to Luc's side and took his arm.

As the men led the way, Ava lingered on the lawn for a

moment. As Max vanished into the darkness, Ava saw a figure slinking down the left side of the abbey, the side where the creek was. It was impossible for her to see who it was.

With a worried glance at the departing Henri, Ava moved toward the abbey. As she walked, she looked behind her. Everyone had vanished into the darkness.

She remembered Henri's warning: *Whatever you do, don't go to the abbey alone.*

Part of her wanted to return to the manor house. But if she did, she'd never know who was walking down its left side.

What if it were Yves? Yves would be able to tell her what was going on. Together, they would solve the case and save his life… and hers. Ava didn't dwell on the alternative: the person creeping next to the abbey was the murderer, and she was walking into a trap

No one had ever solved a crime sitting in a room except Miss Marple. While Ava was British, she was more of a "get out in the field and get your hands dirty" type of sleuth, her love for teacakes aside.

As she neared abbey's left side, the night became darker and the air heavier. It was impossible to see anything. The temperature dropped as she edged her way along the high walls of the ruined edifice. The tall trees that surrounded the abbey were invisible in the darkness. Strange sounds echoed from the night.

At first, Ava jumped every time she heard a sound. Then, she realized that it went with the territory. Anyone walking through a ruined abbey at this hour would hear the sound of the wind and the movement of nocturnal creatures. Remembering that bats were nocturnal, Ava kept her head low.

When she reached the spot where she had seen Steve waiting, she slowed.

Silence surrounded her. Nothing moved. It was as if time had stopped and darkness had swallowed up the person she was following.

Trying to discover where that person had gone, Ava crept forward through the black night. When she entered the woods, the temperature dropped even further. She shivered. Large outcroppings of rocks sprung from the ground. They appeared ominous and mysterious at the same time, like messengers from the underworld.

As she slipped around one of them, Ava turned and eyed the dark walls that soared high into the night behind her.

Was the abbey cursed or haunted as Bea had said?

Hoping that she wouldn't discover the answer to that, she moved through the darkness. She sensed that someone was nearby. It was the same feeling she had had earlier in the garden. This time she didn't call out into the night. If the person following her wasn't Yves or the young man, she didn't want to know who it was.

A sense of acute danger rushed through her. Every part of her body rebelled, screaming that she should leave, but she soldiered on.

A loud cracking sound startled her. Someone dashed through the trees. Ava sprinted after the person. As she ran, tree branches scratched her face and thick bramble cut her ankles. Ava ignored the pain and continued running. When she reached the creek, she slowed.

The person had disappeared, but she could feel their presence.

She walked down to the water's edge. The clouds had parted. The moon now lit the woods. Ava eyed the tall rock formations around her, then turned her attention to the woods on the opposite side of the creek.

Maybe the person had crossed to the other side.

Squinting, she peered out into the dark woods. She saw nothing that indicated anyone was there. Everything was still. The only sound was the sound of the water rippling over the creek's rocky bed.

Suddenly, there was a loud noise. Swinging around to see what it was, she tripped and fell backwards into the creek. The icy water shocked her nervous system. Sputtering, she jumped out and flung herself on the shore.

Shivering, she sat there in her wet clothes.

Everything around her was silent.

Ava stood up. Whoever she had been following was gone. She needed to go back to the manor house. She walked toward the abbey's outer wall. When she reached the spot where she had seen Steve, she paused. If Steve had come here, it was because Yves and the young man were hiding nearby.

For a moment, she contemplated the idea that the young man with the flyers wanted to kill Yves. She immediately abandoned the theory. The others didn't know the young man was here. The only person who knew that was Steve. There must be a reason for the young man's presence. Ava bet that reason was Yves.

Creeping through the darkness toward the manor house, Ava made a plan. Later tonight, she would come back with Henri. Together, they would locate Yves and discover why someone was trying to kill him.

If Yves was still alive...

CHAPTER 20

The abbey and the area around it were shrouded in a damp foglike darkness as Ava hurried across the lawn toward the manor house. Her feet sloshed about in her damp shoes while her wet clothing clung to her body. Shivering, she wrapped her wet hair into an improvised chignon on the back of her head to keep the water from her damp locks from dripping down her back. The fall in the creek had been the second inglorious event in her life as a sleuth. As events came in threes, she couldn't help but wonder what would happen next.

As she neared the manor house, she could see lights coming from the sitting room. Lights were also on in some of the bedrooms.

When she reached the sitting room window, she peered in to get the lay of the land. Kris and Max were the only two in the room. They were standing by the stone fireplace, deep in discussion. From the looks on their faces, it was a serious talk. The others hadn't arrived yet.

Ava continued to the front door. The last thing she wanted was for anyone to see her in her present state. Once inside, she had to move fast. Even if she were to run into someone, she would continue to her room without stopping or explaining why she was wet.

She took a deep breath, gripped the doorknob, turned it and swung the door open in a single movement. In a flash, she entered the house, closed the door behind her and sped across the entrance hall, without looking right or left. She dashed up the steps, taking them two by two, and raced down the hallway to her bedroom.

A door opened. Henri stepped out of his room. He examined the soaked woman in front of him from head to toe. His only reaction was a laconic, "I'll see you for coffee downstairs."

Ava cursed. Henri always seemed to appear when things were going badly for her. On the other hand, this had an upside to it. If things did turn fatal, he would be nearby.

Despite this positive spin, she knew that Henri was upset with her. He had specifically asked her not to go to the abbey and she had. Worse, she had managed to fall into the creek and hadn't discovered anything.

That wasn't true.

She had discovered where they needed to start looking this evening... the spot where the young man had halted and the person she was following had disappeared.

Ava opened her bedroom door, entered and closed it tightly behind her. She hurried to put on dry clothes and shoes.

She ran to the bathroom, took off her wet clothes and jumped into the shower. It was the fastest shower she had ever taken in her life. She stayed there only long enough to wash away the smell of the creek. She dried herself and sprinted into the bedroom to throw dry clothing on. She was thankful that she had brought a second pair of jeans and extra T-shirts. No one would ever know that she had fallen in the creek... no one except Henri, of course, and the person she had been following.

Grabbing socks and shoes, she headed to the chair by the window to put them on. Glancing out, she saw Steve standing in the center of the garden.

What in heaven's name was he doing? Lurking in the garden was becoming a habit with him...

Seconds later, Ava got her response.

The young man darted out of the bushes and spoke to Steve.

Afraid they'd see her, Ava closed the drapes. Peering out through an opening, she watched the two men speak in hurried whispers. When the young man vanished back into the bushes,

Steve turned and returned to the house.

Ava was so excited, she had to stop herself from leaping into the air.

This was a clear example of synchronicity!

Had she not ignored Henri's advice, she wouldn't have fallen into the creek. Had she not fallen into the creek, she wouldn't have had to come up to her room to change. And had she not come up to her room to change, she wouldn't have seen the young man and Steve speaking. If she and Henri were able to follow Steve, he would lead them to Yves.

And now?

Ava shifted from foot to foot as she contemplated her next move.

She needed to speak with Henri alone. Frowning, she realized that if she couldn't, she'd have to follow Steve on her own.

A final thought occurred to her: someone else would be out looking for Yves -- the person who wanted to kill him.

A shiver ran up her spine.

If the person she had followed earlier wasn't Yves or the young man that meant it was the would-be killer. The killer had to be one of the group.

Ava closed her eyes. She tried to remember where everyone had gone after the abbey light show went dark. She had a firm memory of Bea, Luc, Henri and Steve walking off together. But since Steve had a habit of appearing and disappearing, he might have slipped away from the group. She would have to ask Henri. Max had gone to check on the generator, but he could have crossed over to the other side of the abbey first. The person she saw might even have been the missing Lili. Try as she might, Ava couldn't remember seeing Kris or Margot leaving with the group.

She thought back to what she had learned earlier. Arnaud had stumbled upon an unconscious Yves in Italy. He had left him and when he returned minutes later, Yves was gone.

What if Arnaud had warned Yves to stay away from Lili and they had fought? After knocking Yves out, Arnaud left. Feeling guilty, he returned, only to discover that Yves had vanished. He needed to find Yves to prove to Lili that he hadn't killed him.

Or maybe Arnaud thought he had killed Yves and had gone to get a shovel to bury the body. When he returned, Yves was gone. In that case, Arnaud might be here at the abbey to finish off the job.

The more Ava learned, the more the plot thickened and not in a good way.

She swiped on some red lipstick and headed downstairs, ready for anything.

At the bottom of the stairs, she ran into Bea and Luc who were walking down the passageway from Yves's quarters. Luc had his arm around Bea's shoulders.

Bea smiled at Ava. "Did you enjoy the light show?"

Ava nodded. "It was fabulous, absolutely fabulous. But then I'm a pushover for old stones."

"I have a passion for old stones, too," Bea replied with a laugh. "Just not these old stones."

As the trio entered the sitting room, Margot appeared from the kitchen holding a huge Italian espresso coffeepot. "Don't worry, there's another one on the stove," she said, setting it down on the cart.

Ava glanced around. Henri was ensconced in an armchair, chatting with Max. Steve and Arnaud were seated on the couch. Lili was nowhere to be seen, and Kris was standing by the fireplace, alone.

Bea walked over to Max. "What happened to the generator?"

"It's temperamental. It only works when it wants to," Max replied with a deep sigh.

Bea was astonished. "Yves told me he bought a new generator when he installed the light show last year."

"It is new. It's hooked up to the light show control panel. The two machines don't like one another," Max said. "Things break down faster in the countryside."

"Like the bridge?" Henri asked.

Max bristled. "The bridge was due to a lack of

maintenance. Nothing more."

"The abbey is a money pit," Bea said as she settled into an armchair next to Henri and Max. Luc leaned against its edge.

"It's time for coffee," Margot said with a cheerful smile.

She poured coffee into cups while Kris stepped over to the coffee table and began putting profiteroles on plates. With a nervous glance at the door, Arnaud joined her. He picked up plates and began serving everyone. As he made his way around the room, he kept glancing nervously at the door.

When the last person had been served, Lili appeared in the sitting room entrance. Her eyes were puffy and red from crying. She wrung her hands nervously as she stepped into the room. Arnaud smiled at her. She ignored him.

"There's coffee on the cart, Lili," Margot said.

"I didn't come for coffee," Lili replied with a dismissive wave of her hand. She walked to the center of the room and faced everyone. She was now shaking so much that she could barely stand.

"Lili, please," Arnaud murmured. His eyes pleaded with her to stop.

"I have something to say," Lili said dramatically.

Kris stared at her and raised her eyebrows in derision. "Pray tell us what that is."

"I wasn't invited this weekend, but I came anyway. I want

to know which one of you killed Yves."

Max shook his head, weary. "You're talking nonsense, Lili. Yves isn't dead."

"Are you sure?" she asked. She whirled around, looking at each and everyone there as if they were a potential suspect.

Ava didn't like the turn the evening was taking. Glancing at Henri, she could see that he didn't either.

.   "Our last night in Italy, the night Yves disappeared... He had a meeting. He went to it and never returned."

"How do you know that?" Kris asked with a cold stare.

"Because we were together before he left."

"It was probably another woman," Kris said with disdain.

Lili clenched her fists as her face went even redder. "That's not true. Yves loved me. He really loved me. We were going to live together."

Bea shook her head. "My dear, as Yves's wife of over twenty years, I don't doubt that he said he loved you, just as I don't doubt that he is alive. If he were dead, I would know it here," she said, touching her heart. "However, I know that Yves loved you just as he loved the others before you and just as he'll love the others after you. Yves loves the game of love -- the seduction, the chase, and the adoration. He craves adoration. What comes after that, the banal ins and outs of everyday life, is something he likes less. In my long experience, it's something he actively flees. I got more from him than the others because I was Mrs. Yves Dubois. At heart, Yves is very traditional."

Lili narrowed her eyes and raised her voice. She was almost hysterical. "You're wrong. Yves is dead. Arnaud saw the body."

Arnaud slapped his knee. "Lili, stop!"

"You told me you saw him on the ground, unconscious," she said, swirling toward him.

"Unconscious doesn't mean dead," Arnaud countered.

The news hit Bea like a dagger to the heart. She gasped. Luc took her hand. Bea glanced at Henri. He shook his head.

Reassured, Bea swallowed and spoke in a low tone. "Lili, you need to stop. Yves is not dead."

Before Lili could respond, Kris exploded. Crossing her arms, she strode over to Arnaud. "Just what did you see?"

Arnaud paled. "I didn't see anything, Kris."

"You saw something. Tell us," Kris ordered, hovering over him in furor.

Arnaud hung his head and spoke in an almost confessional tone. "Yves left Lili's room and walked up the mountain to the lookout point. I followed him."

Frowning, Max shifted from foot to foot. "What did you see?"

"Nothing. I saw Yves walk up the front of the mountain. I waited halfway down the path. When he didn't come back, I went up to talk with him."

Ava noted that Arnaud didn't mention that Lili had gone up the mountain after Yves.

"What about?" Kris asked with a steely glint in her eyes.

"That's none of your business, Kris," Arnaud responded.

"I think it is," Kris said.

"Then I might ask what you and Max were doing on the mountain," Arnaud countered. "Max and I?" Kris was taken aback.

"You walked up past me, Kris. About fifteen minutes later, Max went by. Neither of you came down. I assumed you took the back path to the hotel."

Kris stared at Max. "Is that true?"

Max nodded. "I did go up the mountain. But then I went up every evening near sunset. I didn't see you. I didn't see Arnaud, and I certainly didn't see Yves, conscious or unconscious."

Lili shook her head vehemently. "Someone attacked Yves. If he's not dead, he's hiding."

Kris glowered at Lili. "If he were hiding, why wouldn't he tell you his whereabouts? After all, you were so close."

"He's going to leave his wife. We're going to live together," Lili said. "I believe him. If he's alive, we'll go away together."

Bea shook her head. "You poor child. You're not the first one he's told that to. Later on, to free himself from his promises, he'll tell you that he couldn't leave me because I'd kill myself if he did."

Luc stood up and spoke to Arnaud. "Did you, or did you not, see Yves unconscious?"

Arnaud sighed. "I did."

"Why didn't you help him?" Margot asked with a cold stare that unnerved Arnaud.

"I felt he deserved it. He'd been playing with people's lives for too long. I just thought someone had punched him out."

"Like you wanted to?" Luc asked.

"Like many of us wanted to," Arnaud replied.

"What did you do then?" Max asked.

"I walked down the mountain. Halfway down, I felt guilty. I went back."

"And then?" Henri asked, insistent.

"Yves was gone. Either he got up and walked away or…"

"Someone threw him into the sea," Lili said. "The police said the coastline is filled with underwater caves. If his body washed into one, it would never be found."

Silent, Ava eyed Steve who was listening attentively. She noticed that he had not volunteered that Yves was alive, nor did he seem upset by what was being said.

"Besides the fact that Yves is alive, why in the world would someone want to kill him?" Kris asked.

Margot turned to Kris, her face pale. "Don't forget what

happened to Gilbert…"

"What does Yves's uncle have to do with this?" Bea asked, perplexed.

"Gilbert announced that he intended to sell the abbey to the regional authorities. A month later, he collapsed and died," Margot said.

"Gilbert had a heart problem," Bea replied, clearly unconvinced.

"I've always wondered if Gilbert's death wasn't provoked by something. We all knew that Yves had fallen in love with the abbey and wanted to keep it. If Gilbert did sell the abbey, what would Yves have done then?" Kris said.

"Are you insinuating that my husband killed his uncle?" Bea asked.

Max turned to Lili, his eyes burning with anger. "You went up the mountain to see Yves."

"I did not," Lili protested. "You're lying."

"Lying? When I came down the back side of the mountain, I stopped to rest. I saw you coming down. I stepped into the bushes to avoid you," Max said.

Arnaud remained silent.

"You're lying. You're lying," Lili said. She burst into tears and ran out of the room.

Annoyed, Max eyed everyone in the room. "We need to remember the work. That's what is important. The work.

Without that, we're lost. This back and forth is destructive. It's not part of the work. The work existed before Yves, and it will exist long after him. The work is timeless."

Margot shook her head. "Without Yves, the work doesn't exist. If he doesn't continue with it, I'm leaving."

"You're welcome to leave at any time," Kris said.

"You have no idea what Yves really thinks of you, Kris. If you did, you'd stop acting like the queen bee," Margot replied.

The room fell silent.

"I suggest we enjoy the profiteroles," Henri said, trying to lighten the atmosphere. "I, for one, have been looking forward to them."

Happy for a respite from the arguing, everyone began to drink coffee and eat.

Ava sipped her coffee. It was Italian espresso. It had a darker, more intense taste than the French espresso she usually drank. She took a forkful of her profiterole. The pastry, custard cream and chocolate sauce melted in her mouth. It was heaven. The darkness of the chocolate complimented the light custard cream. As Ava took a second bite, she heard coughing. She looked up. Kris had turned red and was gagging.

Henri and Max were instantly at Kris's side. She was now doubled over, gasping for breath.

"What is it?" Henri asked.

Max smelled the profiterole on Kris's plate. "Nuts," he

said, looking around the room in panic. "Kris is allergic to nuts."

Bea bounded to her feet. She dashed to the coat rack near the front door, plunged her hand into the pocket of her jacket and took out a pen. She ran over to Kris who could barely breathe.

"Roll up her sleeve," Bea ordered. "Roll up her sleeve."

Max grabbed Kris's arm and rolled her sleeve up. Bea took the cap off the penlike instrument and plunged its tip into Kris's arm. Instantly, Kris began to breathe. After a few seconds, she looked up.

Bea knelt in front of her. "Are you OK, Kris?"

Kris nodded as the redness began to leave her face.

Bea stood up. "There were nuts in the profiteroles. Kris must be allergic like I am. Max, Margot… Help her upstairs. "

"I'll be fine," Kris said in a ragged voice.

Max and Margot each took one of Kris's arms and led her out of the room.

Frowning, Henri sniffed his profiterole and bit into it. "There aren't any nuts in mine."

Luc tasted his. "No nuts."

Arnaud and Steve tasted theirs.

"No nuts," Arnaud said.

"Mine doesn't have any nuts either," Steve added.

Bea who hadn't touched her profiterole handed it to Luc.

He tasted it.

"Nuts!"

"I never eat dessert, so I wouldn't have eaten it," Bea said. "I may be wrong, but someone just tried to kill Kris or me."

Arnaud was on his feet in a flash. "It wasn't Lili. She would never put nuts in profiteroles. In fact, she never bakes with nuts as so many people are allergic to them."

"Anyone could have sprinkled nuts on top of them. However, not everyone would have known who was allergic to nuts. Who served the profiteroles?" Steve asked.

"Kris put them on the plates, and I served them. But I just went around the room in a circle," Arnaud said.

Henri pursed his lips. "It was probably an accident."

"That's impossible," Arnaud protested.

Shaken, Bea stood up. "I am going to retire for the evening. Are you coming, Luc?"

Luc stood up, and the two left.

Visibly disturbed, Steve rose to his feet. "I'm going to turn in for the night, too."

"I don't know who did this, but it wasn't Lili," Arnaud said and stormed out of the room.

Henri and Ava were now alone in the sitting room.

"Who did it, Henri?"

"Anyone could have done it."

"Who were they trying to kill, Bea or Kris?" Ava asked.

Henri raised his eyebrows. "One, both, or none of the above. It's too early to tell. Now will you tell me how you got soaked from head to foot?"

"After the light show, I saw someone heading toward the left side of the abbey. I tried to follow the person but lost them. They vanished near the spot where Steve had been standing earlier.

"And the creek?"

"I fell in on my own," Ava confessed with a wince.

"Some progress is being made," Henri said light-heartedly, in a tone that was belied by the serious expression on his face.

"There's more," Ava said. She told him about Arnaud and Lili's argument. She also told him about Steve and the young man with the flyer.

Henri's frown deepened as he listened.

"What are we going to do?" Ava asked.

"At midnight, we'll meet at the end of the garden and go looking for Yves."

"What's your take on this?" Ava asked.

"Someone is definitely trying to kill Yves. Our only hope of saving him is to find him before his murderer does."

Ava stared at Henri. She had never seen him so serious. "You're not joking."

"If we don't find Yves tonight, he won't be alive tomorrow," Henri replied.

CHAPTER 21

Midnight was an hour and a half away. In order to keep her sanity, Ava piled cups and plates onto the cart in the sitting room and pushed it into the kitchen. She left her own unfinished coffee in the living room for later. The rattling of the dishes reassured her that life continued and that dishes didn't do themselves. As she neared the kitchen, Margot appeared and held the door open for her.

"How is Kris," Ava asked, eyeing the ashen-faced woman.

Visibly exhausted, Margot let out a deep sigh. "Resting. She'll be fine. It was the shock more than anything." Margot walked over to the cart, picked up some dessert plates and carried them to the trashcan. Her mind elsewhere, she scraped the remains of some profiteroles into it. Suddenly, she froze. "Should I have saved them as evidence?"

"Evidence of what? It was just a mistake on Lili's part

although I suspect she'll never admit it," Henri said in a reassuring tone as he entered the kitchen. "It was a good thing that Bea had her adrenaline pen."

"Then it wasn't deliberate?" Margot asked, still not completely convinced.

"Absolutely not. Accidents happen," Henri replied. "If you wanted to kill someone, there are certainly more subtle and effective ways to go about it. *The Case of the Poisoned Profiteroles* sounds like the title of a bad pulp novel."

"I was so worried," Margot said, her voice trailing off. All at once, she burst into tears. "If Yves doesn't come back soon, something bad is going to happen. I can feel it."

"What happened in Italy?" Henri asked as he poured himself some cold coffee from the Italian coffee maker.

Margot took a few seconds to respond. "I have no idea. I seem to be the only person there who wasn't on the mountain that night. I agree with Bea though…"

"In what way?" Henri asked as he studied the expression on her face.

If Yves were dead, I'd feel it," Margot said with emotion.

Hearing whispering and the sound of footsteps, Ava froze. Everything was dark in the ruined abbey. As she moved through the blackness, she could feel danger all around her. Every stone seemed to cry out to her, saying: "Leave while you can."

Ava continued through the obscurity, trying to find some trace of the two men she had followed into the abbey. Overhead, fast moving clouds raced across the night sky, swallowing up the light of the moon and the stars. A soft wind whistled through the ruins blowing up clouds of dust. She covered her mouth to stop from coughing.

All at once, there was more whispering and the sound of footsteps nearby. Instinctively, she moved toward the sounds. In the darkness, she tripped over a stone protruding from the ground. She flew through the air and came down hard on her left side. An unbearable pain rushed through it, causing her to curl up in agony. As she lay there, she felt something sticky spreading under her. She ran her finger over the substance and brought her finger to her face. It was blood.

Ava woke with a start.

The entire left side of her body was numb. Disoriented, she looked at the armchair she had dozed off in and the window next to her. It took her a few seconds to remember where she was. She was in her bedroom in the manor house and was meeting Henri at midnight.

Distraught, she leapt up. *What time was it? Had she overslept?*

She checked the time on the antique bronze clock on the bedside table.

It was 11:40.

She had only been asleep for a few minutes. Frowning, she tried to remember her dream. All she could recall was blood. Disturbed, she checked her fingers. Thankfully, there was no blood on any of them.

Ava stretched and shook her left leg and arm until the numbness went away. She breathed in deeply, bent over and touched her toes. This time, the blood rushed to her head. Fully alert, she stood up straight.

It was time to get ready.

She strode over to her clothes and chose a dry sweater. Her jacket was still wet from her fall in the creek. She had twenty minutes before she was to meet Henri in the garden. She checked the clock to verify that she hadn't set the alarm. She didn't want it to start ringing when she was out and about, alerting people to her absence.

Grabbing her phone from the pocket of her damp jacket, she clicked it on. Nothing happened. The screen remained black. Her fall in the creek had killed her phone. Putting it on the bed, she wondered how she was going to sneak out of the house without being seen.

When Henri had gone to the library to wait, Ava had decided to come up to her room, worried that a late night *tête-à-tête* meeting with him, a man she had just met, would raise Margot's suspicions.

Wrapping a pink leopard print scarf around her neck,

Ava wondered what Margot's role was in everything.

Margot appeared to be the only person who had been at the seminar in Italy and was now at the manor house that hadn't been on the mountain the night Yves disappeared.

Ava didn't know what that meant.

It might be that Margot was the only person no one had seen. The idea of Margot as some master criminal didn't seem plausible. But then no one at the manor house seemed like a killer.

Ava decided to wait for Henri outside. She walked over to the window and looked down at the garden. It was empty.

The moon was almost full. Its bright light illuminated the garden with an eerie silver light. While that meant it would be easier for her and Henri to navigate through the abbey, it also meant it would be easier for someone to see them.

Suddenly, something moved in the garden below. Ava froze and waited. A few seconds later, the young man with the flyers darted out of the bushes. Steve ran up to him. The two men moved across the garden in the direction of the abbey.

Instantly, Ava was out of her room and on the steps, heading downstairs. As she ran by the sitting room, she could see Margot sitting in a chair with a book. Ducking, Ava sprinted to the back door. There was no time to alert Henri. She had to follow the men and see where they were going. Once she discovered where Yves was hiding, she could come back and get Henri.

Ava stepped out into the cool night air and ran across the garden. As the sky overhead clouded over, there was just enough light to keep the men in her sights. By the time they reached the abbey, the clouds completely obscured the moon and the stars. Everything was totally black. And just like in her dream, the men she was following vanished into the dark night.

Standing at the abbey wall, she was frightened. Henri had warned her about coming to the abbey alone. The first time she had fallen in the river. She doubted she would be so lucky a second time. There was no question of stopping. She had no choice. If they didn't find Yves tonight, he would be dead tomorrow.

Ava took a deep breath and slipped through an opening in the wall. Inside the ruined abbey, the immenseness of the space was overwhelming. She stood in the darkness, listening for some sign of the men. As she listened, her ears became attuned to the sounds around her. There was the gentle sound of wind whistling through the ruins, and the low whooshing sound of tree branches brushing against the abbey's outside walls. Every now and then, an owl shrieked. This was followed by the scampering of small animals. Ava listened intently. She had to find the men and Yves before it was too late.

After a few minutes, she heard what she was listening for: the soft sound of movement on the stones and grass inside the abbey.

The sounds were coming from the large space ahead of her. Inching forward, she took baby step after baby step. The last thing she needed was to fall and hurt herself.

The ground was wet with dew, and the night was growing chillier. Ava pulled her scarf tightly around her neck. As she moved, she heard the sound of whispering. Through the darkness, she could make out two figures. She guessed it was Steve and the young man. All at once, she heard another sound coming from behind her. It was the sound of approaching footsteps. The faint light of a flashlight bounced off the stones near her.

Her heart beating wildly, Ava ducked down and slid into a space between two large stones.

As the light grew brighter, she edged forward to see who it was. Peering out of the darkness, Ava caught her breath. The person holding the flashlight was Yves Dubois.

Yves was alive and well!

When Yves reached the center of the large space, he flicked his flashlight on and off three times.

The whispering stopped. The men moved toward Yves.

Suddenly, a gunshot rang out. It echoed through the abbey.

Then everything began to happen all at once.

There was shouting.

People ran off in different directions.

More shots rang out. One ricocheted off a rock near her.

Paralyzed by fear, she forced herself to move. In a burst of adrenaline, she stood up and sprinted through the abbey. A bullet whizzed past her. Panicking, she ran blindly through the dark until she tripped over a rock and went flying through the air. As she came down on the hard ground, an unbearable pain rushed through her left side, causing her to curl up in agony. As she lay there, she felt something sticky spreading under her. She ran her finger over it. She brought her finger up to her face.

It was blood.

Someone grabbed her shoulder with an iron grip. The person put their other hand over her mouth so she couldn't scream.

Ava struggled desperately to free herself. She lashed out at her assailant with her fist until a break in the clouds allowed her to see who the person was... It was Yves Dubois. Blood was dripping from his arm.

She stopped resisting.

"Don't move. We don't want the shooter to find us," Yves whispered.

Ava nodded. He released her.

They could hear someone walking through the stones.

When the person passed close by, Yves turned to Ava.

"When I say run, run to the left. Keep low. Outside, we'll be safer," Yves said.

Terrified of being shot, Ava readied herself.

"Run!" Yves ordered.

In a flash, the two ran to the left. They slid through an opening in the wall and dashed toward the woods as gunshots rang out behind them.

Ava stuck close to Yves as they sprinted through the dark forest. As they ran, branches and bramble cut her face and hands. She ignored the pain and kept running. A bullet hole would feel much worse than any pain she was experiencing.

Abruptly, Yves stopped.

Out of breath, Ava fell to the ground. Yves put his finger to his lips and waited. Everything around them was silent. Whoever had been shooting had lost them.

After a long wait, Yves circled a large rock outcropping and stepped into a space between two rocks. He bent over and brushed tree branches aside, revealing a wooden door built into the ground. Yves surveyed the woods one last time, he then pulled the wooden door open.

He lit his flashlight and shone it downwards. "After you," he said.

Ava stood up and walked to the door. Her left side aching, she climbed down the steep wooden steps into the darkness below. Yves came down after her and pulled the door closed. He barred it with a wooden beam. He pulled on a rope that was on one side of the door. Ava watched him, puzzled.

"It's attached to some brush outside to hide the door."

Yves shone his flashlight over the walls around them. The light revealed a small room with rotted wooden crates piled up high. The room smelled damp and had earth walls propped up with wooden beams. It reminded Ava of her grandparent's vegetable cellar.

Yves walked over to two oil lamps and lit them. He sank to the ground. In the light, Ava could see blood trickling down his arm.

"You've been shot."

Grimacing, Yves ripped open his shirtsleeve. Ava carried the oil lamps over. She put them down, took Yves's flashlight and shone it on his wound.

"I'm no nurse, but there doesn't seem to be a bullet hole. The bullet just grazed you."

"I suppose that's something to be thankful for," Yves said, resigned. All at once, his expression changed. He picked up an oil lamp and held it up to her face. He looked bewildered. "I know you. You're the woman from the book stand, Mr. Sext's niece. What are you doing here?"

"I found your letter. I gave it to Henri... Mr. DeAth. He went to your apartment. Your wife invited him here," Ava explained, glossing over her own subterfuges for being there.

Yves wrinkled his brows, puzzled. "What letter?"

"The letter you hid in my books asking my uncle and Henri DeAth to appraise your library."

"Why would I do that when your uncle is dead?" Yves asked.

Ava caught her breath. "You didn't leave the letter?"

"No..." Yves said.

Suddenly, Ava was angry with herself. She should have known that Yves hadn't left the letter. And just as suddenly, she realized that Henri had known the truth all along.

Standing in a damp root cellar with a gunman on the loose didn't seem like the best time to contemplate what she would say to Henri when she saw him... if she did see him again.

There was the sound of movement overhead.

Yves crept toward the door and listened. The sounds went away. Worried, he turned and strode to the far left corner.

"We have to hurry."

He began to pull crates away from the wall. All at once, he stopped. There was the sound of movement on the wooden door overhead.

Standing in the damp darkness, they both froze. Ava waited with bated breath for the wooden door to fly open and the person with the gun to appear. Instead, the sounds moved away.

Yves frowned. "It was probably an animal."

Ava plunged into the heart of the matter. "Do you know who's trying to kill you?"

Yves gave a strangled laugh. "I have no idea. If I did, I would deal with it. It might be one person or several," Yves said with a sigh. "Until the gunshots, I wasn't totally convinced that someone was trying to kill me."

Ava looked surprised. "Why did you come to my stand then?"

"Benji insisted I go. He'd read about your uncle and Mr. DeAth. Benji was convinced that someone had tried to kill me in Italy."

"Is Benji around twenty-seven, with sandy colored hair and lives in your building?" Ava asked.

Yves nodded. "He's a doctoral student in medieval manuscripts."

"Is he a chosen one?" Ava asked.

Yves burst out laughing. "I'm afraid that's one area where he and I don't see eye to eye. He isn't entirely convinced about the group either. I'm Benji's thesis advisor."

Ava was not reassured by Yves's digressions. If they were to stop the killer, she needed to discover what was going on. "Why are you meeting Steve?"

Yves shook his head. "Steve?"

The American," Ava said.

"Ah... that's what he's calling himself. He's here to buy a manuscript."

"The secret of eternal life?" Ava asked.

"How did you know that?" Yves asked, alarmed.

"Steve mentioned it at dinner."

For the first time, Yves appeared truly worried. "He shouldn't have done that."

"Did you really find a manuscript on eternal life?" Ava asked. She couldn't even wrap her mind around what that would mean.

"Just because a manuscript exists, it doesn't mean what's written in it is true," Yves said enigmatically.

"Why would you sell a treasure like that?"

Yves had a pained expression on his face. "The abbey. I need to pay Bea back."

"Bea is here with Luc," Ava advised him.

Yves looked downcast. "She deserves happiness. I'm not anyone's idea of an ideal husband, and I suspect that won't change. I'm glad Luc is there for her."

"Did you attack Luc in the library?"

"What?"

Suddenly, there was noise on the door overhead again. Both Ava and Yves fell silent. They heard someone slide something across the top of the door. This was followed by another sound: the sound of dripping water.

Yves looked alarmed.

"What's going on?" Ava asked.

Yves didn't answer her. He held his oil lamp up high in the air. Water was seeping in through the wooden door.

"Someone's diverted the stream."

Ava eyed the water that was dripping into the cellar. Yves ran to the stairs and climbed up them. He removed the beam that locked the door from the inside. He pushed up against the door with both hands. It wouldn't move.

"Someone's locked it from the outside!" Yves said as he scurried down the steps. He raced across the cellar to the corner of the room where he had been moving crates earlier.

"Help me," he ordered as he began tossing the rotted crates aside.

Ava helped move the crates. When the last one was gone, Yves crouched down and pushed a wooden plank in the wall forward revealing a small opening. "Take the oil lamp. Go down the steps slowly. They're slippery."

The water was now up washing over their shoes. Without waiting, Ava slipped through the opening and climbed down the rickety steps.

Halfway down, she stopped. Everything was dark. She had never seen a darkness so black. The darkness swallowed up the light from the lamp.

As she continued down, an earthy smell surrounded her. It

was much danker than the smell in the cellar. It smelled of death. As the water dripped down after her, Yves climbed through the opening. He climbed down and handed her his oil lamp. Then he went up the steps again and pulled some rotted crates toward him. He pushed the wooden plank back in place and climbed down the ladder. Water continued to seep through.

"What's going on?" Ava asked, unable to quell the panic inside her.

"The cellar is below ground. Someone opened the sluice in the creek and diverted the water.

"They want to drown us?" Ava asked in shock.

"I'm afraid so. But they don't know about the tunnel. Follow me."

Yves held an oil lamp in one hand and his flashlight in the other. Ava held her lamp up, revealing a tunnel. Roots had broken through the ceiling. The ceiling had collapsed in several places depositing piles of dirt and rocks on the ground. Wooden beams held up the tunnel walls.

"Follow me," Yves ordered.

They hurried through the darkness. The water was now at their ankles. Suffocating from fear, Ava followed Yves without a word. After a while, the water level began to go down until it vanished. They were on dry ground.

"We're going uphill now," Yves said.

As they walked through the darkness, Ava weighed up the number of ways she'd almost died. She couldn't decide which death was worse: dying from a bullet wound, drowning or being buried alive in a rock slide in an underground tunnel.

"Whoever locked the cellar and opened the sluice will assume we've drowned." Yves said.

"How many people know about the root cellar?" Ava asked.

"It's no secret. But it hasn't been used in years."

"And this tunnel?"

"No one knows about it. I only discovered it by accident."

As they advanced, the air became less humid. Ava calculated that they were walking away from the river. After another ten minutes of slow uphill walking, Yves slowed. There were fewer tree roots, and the ceiling was now vaulted. They must be under the abbey.

"You're about to discover the abbey's secret," Yves announced with an enigmatic smile. He stopped in front of a stone door cut into the wall. It had a metal hole in it.

Yves crouched down and picked up an iron bar. He inserted it into the hole and pushed. The door creaked open. A narrow space appeared between it and the stones.

Yves waved Ava through. "The ground has shifted so the door doesn't open completely anymore."

The space was so narrow that Ava has to turn sideways

and pull her stomach in to slide through it. As she went through the opening, the stones scratched her face. Yves handed her the oil lamps, his flashlight and the metal bar. Then turning sideways, he slid through the opening. Once through, he pushed the stone door closed behind them.

They were in a small room with stone walls. The ceiling was arched. An altar stood in the center of the room. It was made from an enormous white stone. Even before seeing the altar, Ava had known that she was in a sacred place.

Holding up her lamp, she spun around in a circle. The oil lamp's flickering light cast odd shadows on the wall.

On one wall, there was a cross that she recognized.

"Is that the Templar Cross?" Ava asked. The Knights Templar was one of the wealthiest and most powerful organizations of Christian military orders in the Crusades. At the beginning of the fourteenth century, the King of France outlawed the Templars and went on to burn many of them at the stake.

"It is," Yves said. He held his lamp high in the air and walked to another wall. He lit up a crude drawing of two knights on one horse. "Here's their symbol."

"Why doesn't anyone know about this?" Ava asked.

"The Templars were known for being secretive. In the end, they were persecuted. They must have hid at the abbey and built the tunnel so they could escape if need be."

"Did the Cistercian monks who built the abbey know about this?"

"The Cistercian monks were linked to the Knights Templar. They had to have known about as this room. It's directly under the abbey's central nave. I suspect that the origin of this room goes back much earlier."

"Pagans?"

"I can't tell you that. I'm not an archeologist. But I believe so."

"Pagans, the Templars, your monks... Why build a temple here? Or an abbey? It's in the middle of nowhere..."

Yves smiled. "Spiritual beings recognize spirituality. It's like a magnet. Notre Dame of Paris was built on a former prehistoric place of worship. Notre Dame is also between two rivers, just like the abbey."

Ava frowned. "Two? I only saw one."

"There's an underground stream behind the garden."

"How did you discover this?"

"I discovered it when the wall in the root cellar collapsed. I explored the opening and found this room. I immediately recognized its importance. I also realized that no one else should know about it. I brought someone in from Paris to repair the wall when everyone was away. The mason never went down the tunnel. I stayed with him to ensure that."

"Is this where you discovered the secret of eternal life?"

Yves burst out laughing. "No."

A noise startled Ava. "Yves, someone's here!"

Yves grabbed the metal bar. He lowered his lamp to the ground. Ava did the same with hers.

From the far end of the room, a figure appeared. Before Ava could see who it was, Yves struck out with his metal bar. The person ducked.

"Careful, you might hurt someone with that," a male voice said.

Ava recognized the voice instantly. "Henri!" she said, lifting her lamp.

Henri DeAth, looking as calm and collected as usual, was standing there, studying the room. He walked over to the cross on the wall and turned. "A Templar Cross? I'm going from surprise to surprise."

Yves lowered the metal bar. "We haven't met. I'm Yves Dubois."

"Henri DeAth," Henri said with a slight bow. He eyed the Ava and Yves. "We've been looking for you for the last half hour."

"How did you find the second opening?" Yves asked.

Ava was surprised. "There's a second opening?"

"In a rock outcrop behind the abbey," Yves said.

"I called Maître Longpont," Henri responded.

Yves nodded. In response to Ava's puzzled look, he

explained, "Mâitre Longpont is the notary who dealt with my uncle's inheritance."

"The Longpont's have been a rich important family in the region for 800 years," Henri said. "If anyone knew the secrets of the abbey, a Longpont would. Mâitre Longpont told me that during a game of hide and seek in the 1920's, his uncle discovered the opening in the rocks. His uncle would come here on his own. He told his nephew about the room before he died."

Yves shook his head in admiration. "I'm astonished Mâitre Longpont told you all that. He's very discrete."

"I was a notary," Henri admitted as if confessing a crime.

Yves smiled. "Now I understand. Just like the Templars, French notaries are a cast apart."

"Perhaps less blood thirsty," Henri said.

"But just as rich," Yves replied.

"Someone tried to shoot us!" Ava said. "Do you know who it was?"

"All hell broke loose after the shots. Steve and Benji, the young man with the flyer, came running toward the manor house. I was outside waiting for Ava. They told me that someone had tried to kill them. The three of us went back to look for you and see if anyone was hurt. We found blood on the ground." Frowning, Henri reached out and touched Yves's arm. "We'll have to deal with that."

"Why didn't you get the others to help you?" Ava asked.

"Because Benji said that this wasn't the first time someone had tried to kill Yves. He suspected one of the group. Max joined us. He heard the shots from the house."

"And the rest of the group?" Yves asked.

"We decided not to wake them unless we found a body… or bodies," Henri admitted.

Ava paled at the thought that one of the bodies might have been hers.

"However, Margot was reading and heard us and came out. She was almost hysterical when she learned what had happened," Henri said.

Yves's expression clouded over.

"You need to tell us what's going on," Henri said to Yves. "Bea and Kris were almost poisoned tonight. Someone put nuts on the dessert."

The news caught Yves by surprise. "Kris and Bea? What have they got to do with this?"

"Maybe it would help if you would explain what "this" is," Henri said staring at Yves.

Yves shoulders slumped.

"Eternal life?" Ava asked.

"Eternal life," Yves confirmed with a brief nod. "It's a manuscript from the Middle Ages. I intend to sell it to pay Bea back."

"It's worth that much?" Henri questioned.

Yves smiled. "Its value depends on how much eternal life is worth to you. However, someone learned what I was doing and is trying to stop me."

"How could they have discovered what you were up to?" Ava asked.

"Someone broke into my email. I only realized it when I saw the email cancelling the seminar this weekend. I had hoped having a larger group here would cover up what I was doing."

"Steve is the buyer?"

Yves nodded. "I had another buyer in Italy. But when he found me unconscious, he pulled out. He said that eternal life wasn't worth dying for." Yves managed a wan smile. "I must say I agree with him."

"We'd better get back to the house before someone else dies," Henri said.

Remembering the discussion about Gilbert and his manuscript, Ava turned to Yves. "Did someone kill your uncle?"

Yves shook his head. "He killed himself. His doctor told him he was heading to a heart attack. But he couldn't give up good wine and rich food."

"Did he leave you the manuscript about the work?" Ava asked.

Yves shook his head. "I never found it."

"How could you teach the work without seeing the manuscript?" Henri asked, intrigued.

"Improvisation. I had gone to three or four of my uncle's lectures. When he died, I repeated what he said and threw in bits and pieces of every esoteric text I had ever read. I had a real knack for it. People believed in the work. People believed in me. As time went on, even I started to believe in the work," Yves said with a sigh. "Being a guru is bad enough, but being a guru who believes what he's selling is worse. That's why I don't blame the person trying to kill me. I'm a fraud. The chosen ones was a gimmick to draw people in. The work is real though. I've seen its effect on people."

"You have no idea who's trying to kill you?" Henri asked.

Yves sighed. "The list is long. When we do discover who it is, I don't want the police involved."

Ava was incensed. "Someone tried to kill you!"

"I probably deserved it," Yves said.

"Maybe you did, but the others didn't," Henri replied.

As they began to leave, Yves turned and looked at the room lovingly. "A few moments here is worth more than eternal life."

Ava glanced at Henri and saw that the expression on his face mirrored Yves' words.

Henri ran his hand over the wall, almost religiously. "I've seen incredible things in my career as a notary but never anything like this."

Yves grasped Henri's arm. "Promise me you won't tell anyone about this room."

"Your secret is safe with us," Henri said.

Ava walked up to the wall and eyed the Templar Cross. Sadness ran through her. She sensed this would be the last time she saw it. But then, she had seen it. Few people could say the same thing.

CHAPTER 22

The manor house was ablaze with lights. A small group of people was standing in front of it. Some held flashlights. Others held oil lamps. When Henri, Ava and Yves appeared out of the darkness, everyone ran toward them. Lili was the first to arrive. Overwhelmed with emotion, she threw her arms around Yves's neck.

I knew you were alive," she said, wiping tears from her eyes.

Luc, Bea, Arnaud and Margot stared at Yves, silent.

Yves gently removed Lili's arms and turned to Bea who was strangely unmoved by his return to life. Seeing the blood on his arm, she pulled it toward her and examined the wound.

"This needs tending to," she said.

When Yves reached out to take her hand, she moved

away. She turned to Ava and Henri. "Where did you find him?"

With a sharp glance at Ava, Henri answered immediately. "We found him wandering near the abbey."

Ava understood immediately what Henri's glance was trying to convey to her. He didn't want anyone to know that she had been with Yves in the root cellar. Only the killer or someone in cahoots with him would know that.

Luc looked at the blood on Yves's arm in horror. "Were you shot?"

"Yes. But the bullet only grazed me," Yves said.

Two figures came running across the lawn from the abbey. It was Max and Kris. When Kris saw Yves she burst into tears.

"I was afraid you were dead," Kris said with real emotion.

Yves put his hand on her shoulder to calm her. "I'm alive. There's no reason to be upset."

"Except someone was out there shooting," Max said, crossing his arms. He eyed everyone. "Which one of you was it?"

Yves took a step toward Max. "Whoever it was isn't shooting now. That's what's important. Let's go inside."

Benji and Steve came dashing up from the far side of the creek. Seeing Yves, Benji ran up and gave him a bear hug. "I didn't think I'd see you alive again."

"I have no intention of dying. If anyone has me in their sights, think again," Yves said in a bad attempt at humor.

"Where were you?" Benji asked.

"In the forest," Yves responded, evasive.

"We looked there. We didn't see you," Kris said with a frown.

"I was hiding. I heard people go by. I didn't know if it was the shooter. I stayed hidden," Yves replied.

"It was pitch-black. In the darkness, you could walk right by someone and not see them," Henri added. "If Ava and I hadn't stumbled onto Yves, we wouldn't have found him."

Max remained silent. His expression was troubled.

The group walked to the manor house. When they reached the front door, Bea addressed them.

"I suggest we meet in the sitting room for coffee in twenty minutes. I'll dress Yves's arm."

"The rest of us can change into dry clothing," Kris replied as she eyed her own soaked shoes and skirt.

Noticing the search party's wet clothing for the first time, Bea frowned. "What happened?"

"The sluice opened and flooded the low land around the abbey," Max said.

"That's dangerous. Did you close it?" Bea asked Max.

Max nodded. "As soon as I saw the water rushing into the low areas by the creek, I knew what had happened. I went and closed the sluice. I had to jam it shut. The locking mechanism was broken."

Kris stared at Max. "Was it deliberate?"

"Hard to say. It might have been an accident or it might have been opened deliberately. The sluice, like the rest of the abbey, needs work. I can only tell you more tomorrow morning when it's light out and I've had time to inspect it."

Standing there, Ava studied the group. The person who had tried to kill Yves was in front of her, and she had no idea who it was. If she and Henri didn't discover the person's identity, they would strike again.

Twenty minutes later, Ava stepped into the sitting room. Arnaud, Lili, Henri, Max, Steve and Benji were the only ones there. No one was speaking. Everyone looked solemn. Only the odor of freshly brewed coffee wafting in from the kitchen added a touch of life to the funereal atmosphere.

Ava eyed the room. Sitting rooms were a mainstay for confessions in Agatha Christie novels. You put all the suspects together in a sitting room and a confession ensued. Looking at the faces around her, Ava sensed that a confession wasn't in the cards. She fervently hoped that no one would die which also was a mainstay in any sitting room scene.

Ava sank down into a chair. She didn't have the slightest idea who was behind the attempted murders. Her first problem was that all the suspects looked normal. She couldn't shake the quaint notion that killers were different from normal people and that this difference was visible to the eye.

Ava's late uncle would have taken great delight in proving her wrong. After all, anyone who watched TV knew that the killer was always the nice neighbor, the friendly postman or the cookie-baking mother. Lacking all three in the present situation, Ava was at a loss.

While she didn't know what had happened on the mountain in Italy, she guessed that the same person who had attacked Yves there had been the one who tried to drown him in the root cellar.

The act was deliberate and meant to be fatal.

She eyed Henri. He was chatting with Max by the fireplace. On the couch, Benji and Steve were also talking. Arnaud sat next to them, silent. Seated in a comfortable armchair, a tense Lili clutched a throw pillow, white-knuckled. She ignored Arnaud's pleading glances. Luc entered and made a beeline for Henri and Max. He was visibly on edge.

Ava studied the suspects. This was her last chance to discover who did it. She ran over her suspect list one final time.

Suspect 1: Lili. Ava eliminated her right off the bat. Lili was in love with Yves. Why would she kill him? Although now that he had rebuffed her in front of everyone, all bets for the future were off.

Suspect 2: Arnaud. He desperately loved Lili. Try as she might, Ava couldn't see him as a killer. He just didn't have it in him. Besides, he had only come to the abbey to prove to Lilli that Yves was alive.

Suspect 3: Kris. Kris's life was the work. Yves embodied the work. The expression on her face when she had seen him this evening, alive and well, was one of love and admiration. It was not the reaction of a killer. Plus, someone may have attempted to kill her with a profiterole.

Suspect 4: Max. Max loved the abbey. To remain here, he needed Yves alive. If Yves died, Bea would decide the abbey's future, and there was little doubt as to what that decision would be. It was possible that Max had tried to kill Bea with the profiterole and poisoned Kris instead.

Suspect 5: Bea. Hers was a classic situation... the abandoned wife, the lover, a distant husband and money at stake. Bea had every possible motive. However, she still loved Yves and would never kill him. Ava removed her from the list.

Suspect 6: Luc. The lover was the ideal suspect. However, Henri had hit the nail on the head when he said that Luc needed Yves alive so that Bea could divorce him.

Suspect 7: Benji. Ava looked up and studied him. This was the first time she had time to look at him closely. He had candid features and was extremely good-looking. In addition, he had helped the universe choose Ava and was helping Yves. He didn't seem like someone playing a double game, moving from trusted friend to cynical killer in the flash of an eye. Plus, he hadn't been in Italy.

Suspects 8 and 9: Margot and Steve. They were the wild cards. Margot was hiding something. Margot might have been having an affair with Yves, but she didn't seem particularly upset over his relationship with Lili. That left Steve. He wanted to buy the manuscript. Would he rather kill than pay for it? However, a killer would probably have fixed his glasses before going on a shooting spree.

All in all, in Ava's opinion, none of them could have done it. Things would be much easier if someone would just stand up and confess.

Margot pushed the rattling cart into the room. Kris followed her in with two large Italian espresso makers, one in each hand. Several people looked up nervously as they entered the room.

Hadn't rattling come before a near death just hours earlier?

"I made the coffee myself. It's fine," Margot said in response to the unasked questions that hung in the air. She held up a package of cookies. "I just opened it." Like earlier, she poured the coffee while Arnaud served everyone.

"Coffee is just what we need," Bea said as she entered the room followed by Yves whose arm was covered with a white bandage. Luc shifted on his feet nervously. Bea walked directly over to him and put her hand on his arm. With a look of relief, Luc closed his hand over hers.

While Margot poured coffee for the latecomers, Yves strode to the center of the room.

"First, a warm welcome to those of you I don't know. I only had a few brief seconds to speak with Henri and Ava. I haven't had the pleasure to speak with Steve yet. We all welcome you here." Yves eyed Ava. "You are a chosen one. You are very fortunate indeed."

Ava was puzzled. Hadn't Yves said in the temple that he didn't believe in the chosen ones? Why was he still pretending he did?

"It's time to clear the air and discover what's going on. What we learn in this room will stay in this room. There will be no police..." Yves said as his eyes went from person to person.

Lili leaned forward, on the verge of tears.

"But whatever is going on has to stop. Do we all agree?" Yves asked.

Anger shot across Bea's face. "If someone is trying to kill you, we need to inform the police."

"I'm alive. I intend to stay alive. As for the past, I believe in letting bygones be bygones. The work means that we need to forgive and move on. Anger and animosity are the work's enemies," Yves said in a calm tone. His body language was that of a man in control.

Henri shook his head in disagreement. "You're on a very dangerous path, Yves. What's to stop the person who tried to kill you from killing you later? That person might even kill one of us. Kris almost died earlier."

"It won't happen," Yves said in a voice that brooked no dissent. "Now let's get started. Does anyone here know who tried to kill me?"

A silence fell over the group.

"It wasn't me," Arnaud said to Lili.

Lili ignored him. Her eyes were on Yves, begging him to look at her.

Leaning against the fireplace, Max shifted his weight. "If we're going to get to the bottom of this, we need to start at the beginning. What was going on in Italy?"

A pale Lili rose to her feet. Barely able to stand, she spoke directly to Yves. "You said you were meeting someone. You never came back. I thought you were dead."

Yves eyed Lili with sorrow. "I'm sorry. I should have contacted you, but I didn't know who was trying to kill me. It could have been anyone who was in Italy. I couldn't take that chance."

Devastated, Lili sank back into her chair. "I would never hurt you... Never. I'd kill myself first."

Yves walked over to her. "Lili, there's no question of that. You are important to me. You are important to the work."

"What did you see on the mountain?" Kris asked.

"I was meeting someone. Unfortunately, when the man

arrived, I was unconscious. Someone had hit me on the head. The man I was meeting helped me down the mountain. I came back to France and hid. Only Benji knew where I was."

Bea watched her husband and didn't say anything. Luc was also silent.

"Are you leaving us? Leaving the work?" Lili asked.

Kris's expression changed abruptly. "No one said anything about Yves leaving the work." She swirled toward him. "You wouldn't do that?"

In response, Yves remained silent. His silence spoke louder than any words could. Kris's face clouded over.

Arnaud rose to his feet. "I followed you up the mountain, Yves. I need you to tell Lili that I wasn't the one who attacked you. She believes it was me."

"I have no idea who attacked me. I doubt strongly that it was Arnaud," Yves responded.

"But it might have been," Lili said with a pointed look at Arnaud.

"Yes, it might have been," Yves admitted.

"Except it wasn't," Arnaud replied in a virulent tone.

Henri spoke up. "I wasn't in Italy. So I don't have any preconceptions about what happened there. It might help if I led the questions."

"I accept. Remember, what is said in this room stays in this room," Yves insisted.

Henri nodded and turned to Arnaud. "Why did you go up the mountain?"

"I wanted to speak with Yves and convince him to tell Lili the truth."

"Stop Arnaud!" Lili said, red-faced.

"He's not going to run away with you, Lili. It's naive to think he will," Arnaud replied.

Bea stared at Yves. "Tell her the truth."

Yves turned toward Lili once again. "Lili, you are a special person in my life. I'm just not made for living with someone. Bea can attest to that. Please accept my honesty and move on with your life."

Lili began to cry.

Yves walked over to Luc and Bea. "I want you to be happy... both of you. I haven't been a good husband, Bea. I'm sorry."

Bea reached out and touched Yves's arm with tears in her eyes. She then took Luc's hand in hers and clutched it tightly.

Arnaud spoke up, eyeing Max and Kris. "What were you doing on the mountain?"

Defensive, Kris crossed her arms. "I wanted to speak with Yves."

"About what," Henri asked in a very non-confrontational tone.

Kris sighed. "It was about the manuscript. I wanted to

know if Yves intended to sell it."

"What manuscript?" Bea asked, puzzled.

Steve leaned forward and stared at Yves, waiting for his answer.

"The manuscript on eternal life," Yves responded. "And the answer is yes. It's mine. I can do what I want with it…"

Kris erupted in anger. "The manuscript belongs to the abbey. The abbey is the source of the work. Therefore, the manuscript belongs to the work. No one is bigger than the work, Yves…. No one."

Yves remained calm. He ignored Kris's anger and responded in a neutral tone. "The manuscript is mine. The abbey is mine. I inherited from Gilbert. My uncle didn't leave the abbey to the group. He left it to me. Do you know why? Because I am a master."

His words had an almost hypnotic effect on Kris. Once again, she slipped into her role of the true believer.

"When he chose you for the work, he was right. Without you, the work would not have spread like it has. But that doesn't give you the right to sell the manuscript!" Kris said in a begging tone.

Max put his hand on Kris's shoulder. "That's enough, Kris," he said gently.

Margot jumped to her feet. "Your uncle Gilbert fell down the steps. How do we know his death wasn't an accident?"

"That's ridiculous, Margot," Yves said. "My uncle was warned his heart wasn't strong enough to climb stairs, and he continued to do so. He smoked and drank. It's amazing he lived as long as he did." His expression showed that the subject was closed.

"What happened to you in the abbey tonight? Who fired the shots? Who opened the sluice?" Bea asked.

"I went to meet Steve and Benji. As I walked toward them, shots rang out. There was chaos. We all ran. I hid in the root cellar. Someone locked me in and opened the sluice. I almost drowned."

"How did you get out?" Kris asked, wide-eyed.

Henri raised his hand. "Ava and I let him out. When we were looking for Yves, we heard banging on the root cellar door. I opened it and Yves climbed out. We then walked back to the abbey."

Margot paled. "The root cellar is below ground. If you open the sluice, the whole area floods. You could have died. First, there was the bridge. Then the profiteroles. And now we have gunshots and a flooded root cellar. What's next?"

"Nothing is next," Yves said. He eyed Bea. "I'm sorry to have brought you into this."

Max stepped forward. "Kris almost died. Bea could have died, too. I want to know why? Which one you did it?" He spun around and glared at Lili. "Lili?"

Lili shook her head. "I don't cook with nuts."

Max's eyes narrowed. "They got onto the profiteroles somehow."

"Max, leave Lili alone. There were nuts in the kitchen. It could have been anyone of us," Margot said.

Henri nodded. "The nuts might have been an accident. If they were meant to kill either Kris or Bea, it was badly thought out. The gunshots were a different story. They could have been used as a warning. But whoever locked Yves in the root cellar meant it to be fatal."

The room fell silent.

Ava eyed the suspects. Now was the time for someone to confess.

Instead Yves spoke.

"I intend to sell the manuscript on eternal life and pay Bea back. That way the abbey is safe."

"You won't be involved in the work anymore?" Margot asked.

Yves turned toward her, totally calm. "No. I won't. It's time for someone else to take the reins. Margot, Kris, Max... Anyone of you could do it.

Margot shook her head. "If you leave, I'm leaving, too."

Kris sneered. "Yves is more important to you than the work?"

Margot stared at Kris coldly. "Yves was the work to me.

His uncle opened a door. Yves helped me go through it. If he leaves, I'll continue on my path alone. I'm ready."

Arnaud was incensed. "The work?! There's a killer on the loose, and all everybody can talk about is the work!"

Kris wheeled around and glared at Arnaud. "The only reason we're here is because of the work. To me, that's all that counts."

"Did you ever see the manuscript about the work?" Margot asked Yves.

"Gilbert showed it to me once. But I never saw it again," Yves said.

"But you read it?" Margot asked.

Yves didn't answer her.

Bea eyed Yves. "You owe me three million euros. Steve is charming, but I doubt he has that type of money."

Yves looked at Steve. "Are you going to tell them who you are?"

Steve sighed and pushed his taped glasses up his nose. "I work in tech. Let's just say that I've been very lucky. Three million euros is well within my means. I intend to gift the manuscript to my foundation."

"So you're really leaving the work?" Kris asked Yves.

"Yes. My time has ended. When I came down the mountain, I realized that while I might have been chosen to lead the work, the attack was a sign that it was time for me to stop."

"Kris, I saw you down by the sluice. What were you doing there?" Benji asked with a cold stare.

Kris didn't speak. Her face turned pale. Max put his hand on her shoulder.

"Kris. We have to tell them the truth."

Ava was so startled by this turn of events that she almost fell out of her chair.

The confession in the sitting room! Who said these things only happened in books?

Yves eyed Max. "We're waiting."

Max's shoulders slumped. He spoke directly to Yves, ignoring the others. "I was angry about the abbey. I was worried you'd sell it. At first, I just wanted to scare you."

"Flooding the root cellar was more than a threat," Yves said.

Max sighed. "I know. I intended to let you out. When I went back, you were gone."

Kris shook her head. "Max…"

"I'm sorry, Kris. It was stupid. But the abbey is my life. I couldn't imagine losing it."

Without a word, Kris turned on her heels and left the room.

"Max. Thank you," Yves said. "That wasn't easy to do." Yves walked over and hugged him. "It's over. We won't talk about it again."

Without a word, people began to wander off.

Watching them, Ava understood that something had ended with Max's confession: the illusion that being a chosen one would protect you from the world.

Steve hurried over to Yves. "Can I see the manuscript now?"

"Let's leave it till tomorrow," Yves replied. "It's been a long day."

He and Steve walked off together.

Ava and Henri were the only two left in the sitting room. She noticed that Henri was still on edge. "Are you OK?"

Henri frowned. "I'm not a fan of happy endings," he said, shaking his head.

Kris entered with two cups of coffee. "I just reheated the coffee. Who would like some?

"I'd love some," Henri said, taking a cup.

Ava shook her head. "I still have my coffee from earlier. Thank you."

Kris left.

Henri raised the cup to his lips and then put it down. "I'll wait until it cools."

Ava handed Henri her cup. "Take mine. It's cold though."

Henri took her coffee and drank it down. "Tonight is going to be a long night," he said cryptically and left the room.

Ava went into the kitchen. Kris was sitting alone at the kitchen table.

"Are you OK?" Ava asked.

"I'm just tired," Kris said. She looked away and continued sipping her coffee as if she were alone.

Unnerved by the woman's odd behavior, Ava left the kitchen and went upstairs.

They had found the killer, but somehow she didn't feel as happy as she should be feeling. She couldn't pinpoint why. She sighed. The important thing was that Yves was alive and that no one else had died.

CHAPTER 23

With the early morning sun streaming through her bedroom window, Ava woke and opened her eyes. For the first time in ages, her sleep had been dreamless. She didn't know if that was good or bad. As she sat up in bed, the sound of a wailing siren startled her. In seconds, she was on her feet. She threw on some jeans, pulled a sweatshirt over her pajama top and raced out into the hallway, bare-footed.

Bea, Luc, Henri, Yves, Max and Margot were all standing below in the manor house entrance in various states of undress.

Ava sprinted down the stairs toward them. "What's happened?"

Emotionless, Henri turned to her. "Kris tried to kill herself."

Ava was shocked.

Bea took charge. "Let's go into the kitchen. I'll make coffee."

Minutes later, everyone was sipping coffee silently around the kitchen table.

"When I heard the roar of the motorcycle leaving, I woke up," Margot said. Her eyes were red from crying.

"Lili and Arnaud took the motorcycle and left in the middle of the night," Yves explained.

"After they tried to kill Kris?" Ava asked.

Margot shook her head. "No. Kris tried to kill herself. When I heard the motorcycle, I peeked in all the rooms to see who had left. Lili and Arnaud's rooms were empty. Kris's room was also empty. I came downstairs and found her sitting on the couch, unconscious. An empty coffee cup was next to her. She had a suicide note on her lap. There was also a second note. In it, she apologized for the other death."

"Other death?" Ava asked, alarmed. She looked around the kitchen to see who was missing. "Are Benji and Steve OK?"

"They're fine," Henri said. "I'm the one she thought she'd killed." He eyed everyone at the table. "Kris offered Ava and me coffee last night. Ava refused. I accepted. The coffee was too hot to drink. This morning, I smelled it. Bitter almonds..."

"Cyanide?" Ava couldn't believe her ears. "Why would

Kris do that?"

Henri turned to Max. "Maybe you can tell us?"

Max lowered his head, defeated. "It was Kris who tried to kill Yves in Italy. I arrived and stopped her. When Yves disappeared, we both believed he'd wandered off dazed and had fallen off the mountain."

"That's why Kris pretended to speak with Yves on the phone," Margot said. "She really believed he was dead."

"And that she had killed him," Henri added.

The gravity of what was being said hit Ava like a ton of bricks. Kris had tried to kill her, too!

Steve and Benji entered the kitchen. Their expressions showed that they were aware of Kris's suicide attempt.

Max nodded. "I realized early on that Yves was alive but decided not to tell Kris. I didn't know what she would do if she learned that." Max turned to Yves. "I tried to warn you. I followed you to the quay."

"You were the one on the motorcycle?" Ava asked, astonished.

"That was me," Max admitted.

"Max was the one who pushed you into the Canal St. Martin," Benji said.

Ava stared at him, astonished.

"I wouldn't have let you drown," Benji said. "If the others hadn't jumped in to rescue you, I would have done it myself. Luckily, Henri was also there."

"Why did you push me?" Ava asked Max.

"I saw you spying on Margot and Kris. I wanted to warn you to stay away. Kris had become more and more unhinged after Italy. It was impossible to reason with her," Max said with a sigh.

Henri sat back in his chair. "And the bridge?"

"Me again," Max confessed.

Yves put his coffee cup down. "What happened last night, Max?"

Max sighed. "Kris was furious that Bea was here. When she learned that you were alive, she went over the deep end. She realized that the work would end. She lashed out wildly to defend the abbey and the work."

"She didn't really mean to kill me," Yves said to the others. "She was just angry."

Henri shook his head. "Don't fool yourself, Yves. She meant to do it."

"But why?" Yves asked. "Was the work that important to her?"

Margot spoke in a low tone. "She'd become obsessed by it. Anyone or anything that got in its way had to go."

"She decided that Henri and Ava were enemies of the work. That's why she tried to kill them," Max said, contrite.

"What are you going to do now?" Bea asked Yves.

"I don't know..." Yves responded.

"Where was the poison?" Luc asked.

"In the last pot of coffee she made," Bea said. "When I washed it out, I smelled bitter almonds."

"When the police come, what are you going to say?" Luc asked Yves.

"I know the police chief. He'll believe me when I tell him Kris was unhinged. She left a note. As for the second note, as far as I'm concerned it never existed. Do we all agree?"

Everyone remained silent.

Ava looked at Henri. If she hadn't offered him her coffee last night, he might be dead. A shiver ran through her.

Steve stepped forward. "I'm still interested in buying the manuscript."

Margot eyed Yves. "Are you going to tell him or should I?"

Steve's whole demeanor changed. His cool hipster persona vanished, replaced by the look of a shrewd businessman. "Something happened to it?"

"We found ashes in Kris's room," Margot said. "I had hidden the manuscript in my room. She found it sometime yesterday and burned it."

Steve turned pale. "No!"

"I'm afraid so," Yves said.

Steve was devastated. "Do you have a copy?"

"Of course," Yves replied.

Benji stared at Yves. "Maybe it's time to tell everyone the truth, Yves."

All eyes turned to Yves.

"My uncle was a wonderful scholar. He collected ancient manuscripts. Most were your run-of-the-mill manuscripts. They didn't contain secrets, magical formulas or anything really earth-shattering that people would spend fortunes on. However, my uncle was blessed with a wonderful imagination and a great sense of synthesis."

"What did he do, Yves?" Bea asked.

"He created manuscripts. He chose subjects people would pay fortunes for, wrote manuscripts on them and made the manuscripts look ancient."

"Forgery?" Steve asked.

"In a sense. The text was original. It was just the origin that he fudged. He was gifted at that. He used old manuscripts as a base, bleached the paper and wrote the text... That's how he paid for the works to the abbey."

Steve stared at Yves. "There never was a manuscript on eternal life?"

"There was a manuscript. My uncle wrote it. He took the best of everything he had read on the subject and created his own."

Margot was devastated. "Then there never was a

manuscript about the work and the chosen ones?"

Yves shook his head. "No. That manuscript was all in his mind. But he executed it as if it existed and set it in motion. The result was the group. Sometimes, ideas take on a life of their own."

Max was stunned. "But I felt it. I lived it. The work changed my life."

"I didn't say the work was a fraud, just that the ancient manuscript that revealed its secrets never existed."

Margot laughed. "I thought I'd been chosen by the universe."

Deadly serious, Yves stared at her. "You were. We're alive. Don't forget that. Sometimes, people need an ancient manuscript to understand why they're here. But just watching the sun rise in the sky every morning should tell us that we're all chosen ones. Isn't the abbey and its forest proof of that?"

For an instant, Ava was disappointed that Yves was giving up the work. Listening to him, she felt inspired.

Bea sighed. "What are we going to do about the money you owe me, Yves?"

Yves sighed. "If the regional government still wants to buy the abbey and its land, I'll sell it to them."

Steve took a sip of coffee. "What if I bought it?"

"The abbey?" Yves asked, astounded.

"Wandering around the ruins last night, I felt something

incredible. It shook me to my core. I'd like to know the abbey was here when I needed to feel that again. The group can continue to use it," Steve said with a glance at everyone.

Yves shook his head. "The group has to end. It's time for everyone to go out on their own."

Steve nodded. "I understand." He turned to Max. "I'll need someone to take care of it. You know the abbey better than anyone. Would you like to do that?"

Max was so moved that he couldn't speak.

"There's something that's been puzzling me. If you're worth millions, why are your glasses taped?" Ava asked Steve.

Frowning, Steve took his glasses off and examined them. "I sat on them on the airport bus. If I wanted to catch the train, the only option was tape."

"I thought you were a broke student," Ava admitted sheepishly.

"I was one once," Steve said. He pointed at his glasses and smiled. "Old habits die hard."

Henri eyed Luc. "Now can you tell us what startled you in the library?"

"Like I said, I heard a noise and fell. When Bea believed it was Yves, I liked the fact that she was so protective of me. I didn't protest as much as I should have," Luc admitted.

Bea took his hand.

Henri turned to Benji. "You're the one who left the letter

in Ava's stand." It was a statement, not a question.

Benji nodded. "That was me. When Yves ran off, I wrote up a letter, went back to the stand and stuck it in a book, hoping you'd find it. I even went there the next morning to discover the letter myself, but someone had beat me to it."

"I'm glad you did involve Ava and Henri. Without Sext and DeAth, I'd probably be dead," Yves said. He turned to Ava. "I never met your late uncle, but he would be proud of you."

Bea eyed Max. "Who put the nuts on the profiteroles?"

"Kris. She did it to draw attention away from her and to warn you to leave the abbey's secrets alone."

"Does the abbey have a secret?" Bea asked.

Yves smiled enigmatically. "Secrets are to be discovered... If the abbey has one, I'm confident Steve will find it."

Epilogue

It was a beautiful day in May, one of those days that made you glad to be alive. With a smile, Ava ran her hand over the green boxes of her paradise as she organized the books in her stand, taking delight in each and every one. Who would have thought that a tatty copy of *War and Peace* would bring her such joy? She glanced down at Henri who was deep in discussion with three blue turbaned Sikhs. Ali was leaning against his stand holding a drawing pad in one hand and a pencil in the other, sketching to his heart's delight.

Tourists, delighted to be in the city of love, wandered down the sidewalk, stopping here and there to buy a book or a postcard.

Ava closed her eyes and breathed in the joy around her. When she opened them, Benji was going through the books in her stand. He had a skateboard under one foot.

"Benji!" Ava said.

He turned to her. "I'm glad to see you again," he said with a grin.

Ava was happy to see him, happier than she would like to admit. It had only been ten days since the events at the abbey, but it seemed like ancient history. She was now not only Ava Sext, a bookseller on the Seine. She was also part of the sleuthing duo, Sext and DeAth. This thrilled her. Not that she wanted to solve crimes all the time. Bookselling was a perfectly fine everyday profession.

"How are things at the abbey?" Ava asked.

"Everyone is gone except Max. Henri came last weekend and helped Yves chose which books to sell."

"And Kris?"

"She's left the hospital."

Ava was alarmed. "Escaped?"

Benji shook his head. "No. She's gone to live in the cloistered spiritual community that she belonged to before she joined the work. Yves warned their leader about her. He's sending her to their most isolated community."

Ava breathed a sigh of relief. "I'm glad to hear that. What are you up to?"

Benji moved his foot back and forth on his skateboard as he spoke. "I'll be in Paris all month. Then I'm moving to New

York to get my doctoral degree."

"I'll be here all month, too," Ava said, unabashedly forward.

"You're lucky. There's so much to do in Paris. There's a concert in two days on a boat on the Seine. The band is great."

"Well, well... who do we have here?" Henri said as he joined them.

"I wanted to thank you. Without you and Ava, Yves would be dead," Benji said.

"If you hadn't pushed Yves to come here and written the letter, he would be dead," Henri replied.

"I've got to get going," Benji said. He jumped on his skateboard and made a small circle on the sidewalk. "Have a good afternoon!" He rolled off down the quay with a wave.

Ava frowned, annoyed.

Henri eyed Ava with concern. "What is it?"

"I'm vexed. Benji told me he's here all month and raved about a great concert in two days. He didn't invite me."

Henri raised his eyebrows. "Why would he ask you to go?"

Ava was incensed. "Why wouldn't he? Is there something wrong with me?"

"Not at all," Henri replied and burst out laughing.

Ali came over and joined them. "What's so funny?"

"Nothing," Ava replied.

To her annoyance, Henri remained in place watching her as if waiting for something.

Suddenly, Ava understood.

Her stand.

She turned and went through the books. The envelope was at the end of the first row of books. Ava took it out and opened it.

"What is it?" Henri asked.

Peering over Ava's shoulder, Ali answered for her. "It's a ticket to a concert."

Ava clutched the ticket, smiling.

"It seems that Sext and DeAth will be reduced to DeAth for one evening," Henri said with a chuckle.

"If I find a dead body, you'll be the first person I'll contact," Ava replied.

Ali took a crumpled piece of newspaper out of his pocket. "Do you want to hear your horoscope, Ava?"

"No!" Ava said. "From now on, I'm going to write my own horoscope. After all, I'm a chosen one."

"How much is this?" a spiky haired woman asked Ava. She held up a pair of green frog salt and pepper shakers.

Pulling her shoulders back, Ava strode over to the woman and began bartering. Life was back to normal and Ava couldn't be happier.

Preview of "Death in the Louvre"

The sky over Paris was a pale shade of grey. It was a pearl grey with large swathes of pink and yellow splashed through it. The early morning June sky promised a warm sunny afternoon. For the moment, cotton-candy clouds drifted peacefully across it. The clouds moved so slowly that the sun played hide and seek with them: popping out in a glorious beam of light only to disappear behind the next fluffy mass.

When bright rays of sunshine came pouring into the Café Mollien in the Denon Wing of the Louvre Museum, Ava Sext was in heaven. Seated at an alcove table directly in front of a huge antique window that gave onto the Carrousel Garden across the road, she watched the sunlight dance on *Arc de Triomphe* at the garden's entrance. The gold leaf on its statues glittered in the bright light just as it must have two hundred years earlier when the arch was built to commemorate Napoleon Bonaparte's military victories

Like a cat basking in the sun, Ava leaned back in the warm sunshine. Two hundred years ago, who could have imagined that she -- Ava Sext, born and raised in London -- would one day be enjoying the scene over a late breakfast? And that she would be enjoying it as a Parisian…

Ava pushed her long brown hair behind her ears. Dressed in loose-fit jeans and a chic blue top by an Italian designer, she had a magenta-colored leopard print chiffon scarf jauntily wrapped around her neck, fuchsia pink sports shoes on her feet and a touch of bright red lipstick on her lips. The rest of her heart-shaped face was makeup free. Anyone looking at her would think she was French.

"Cappuccino, a double espresso, cheesecake and an apple tart," a tall man said, setting a tray down on the table in front of her.

With a smile, Ava looked up at Henri DeAth who was looking especially dapper that morning. He was wearing dark jeans and a pale blue shirt that made his blue eyes look even bluer. A charcoal grey sweater was thrown over his shoulders. Salt and pepper hair curled around his face like a halo. In his sixties, Henri had the youngest spirit of anyone she had ever met.

Henri had been friends with Ava's late Uncle Charles. After an inheritance, Charles Sext, a New Scotland Yard detective, had quit his job and moved to France to run an outdoor book stand on a Parisian quay overlooking the Seine River, having decided to enjoy life far from crime and criminals. However, sleuthing was in his blood. Before his death last year, he and Henri had solved several crimes together that had brought them some renown.

"A sunny day. A perfect day to visit the Louvre," Henri announced. "What tourist in his right mind would want to spend such a glorious day in a dusty museum?"

Having seen hundreds of people lined up at the pyramid entrance to the Louvre, Ava knew there were quite a few.

As Henri slid into the seat across from her, Ava, hungrier than she would like to admit, removed the items from the tray and spread them across the table.

"What do you want?" she asked, trying to keep her gaze off the apple tart that was screaming her name. The cappuccino was also calling out to her.

"Ladies' choice," Henri replied, always the gentleman.

"You go first," Ava said, hoping that he would ask for the cheesecake.

Henri raised his eyebrows. With an amused smile, he pointed at the tart and the cappuccino. Ava's heart sank.

"Those are for you. But if you prefer the cheesecake and espresso, I'll be happy to change," Henri said.

"No. I accept my fate," Ava replied with a grateful grin. She pulled the apple tart and cappuccino toward her before he changed his mind.

Henri rolled his eyes over the café's soaring ceilings, massive stone pillars and the ornate monumental staircase that led up to the café from the ground floor. "This is quite a change from Café Zola."

Café Zola was on the *Quai Malaquais* on the left bank of the Seine River in the center of Paris. Across the street from his book stand, the café was Henri's daily coffee and lunch spot. It was a traditional café where the waiters wore long white aprons over their dark trousers and were known to be grumpy on occasion. If Ava were honest, they were grumpy on a daily basis. But that was part of Café Zola's charm.

"When are Gerard and Alain going to reopen?" Ava asked, trying to hide the worry in her voice. Gerard and Alain were the two cousins who owned Café Zola. Gerard dealt with the customers while Alain spent his time in the café's tiny kitchen, whipping up unforgettable meals. The café had closed for works after a water leak.

"In two weeks. They've decided to renovate," Henri answered, taking a sip of his espresso.

"Renovate!" Ava repeated, horrified. "You mean modernize?" Images of neon lights and brightly-colored hip furnishings appeared before her eyes.

"Gerard and Alain? Modernize... Never. They don't even know what the word means. They're just "freshening up" the decor."

Ava furrowed her brow, not at all reassured by the term "freshening up".

Henri gestured at Café Mollien's lavish ornamentation. "This as an opportunity to spend time in the Louvre. We see it every day from our book stands, but I can't remember the last time I was here. Until Café Zola reopens, we can have breakfast here and see some art at the same time."

"That leaves lunch," Ava said, taking a bite of her tart. It melted in her mouth. Its sweet crust contrasted perfectly with the apples' tartness.

Watching her, Henri burst out laughing. "For a skinny English girl who arrived last year, you've turned into quite the French gourmet."

"That's your fault and Alains," Ava replied, content.

The first time Ava had gone to Café Zola, she had ordered a sandwich for lunch. Alain was so upset that he marched out of the kitchen to see what was wrong. The sandwich was quickly replaced by a *coq au vin*, rooster in wine sauce, and a *tarte tatin*, a caramelized upside down apple tart, for dessert. It was delicious. It was also life-changing. Ava's sandwich days were behind her.

Gazing blissfully at her surroundings, Ava smiled. "I never thought I'd go to work and see the Louvre every day. In London, my office looked on a brick wall with dripping blood painted on it."

Thinking back to her career in London, Ava shuddered. A communication specialist in a boutique PR firm, her days and nights had been devoted to posting social media posts and tweeting for her celebrity clients. She realized it was time to leave when she had gone on a drunken tweeting frenzy after a romantic relationship had ended badly, and no one had noticed. In fact, some clients had even complimented her on the originality of her tweets!

Seeing the expression on her face, Henri misread her thoughts. He nodded as he bit into his cheesecake. "I agree. These pastries don't hold a candle to Alain's desserts, but we have to eat."

Ava took a sip of her cappuccino and studied the mass of humanity that was hurrying up the staircase to the Grand Gallery. People rushed by without breaking pace. Since she and Henri had arrived, the crowds coming up the stairs had grown denser.

"Where are they all going?" Ava asked, curious.

"To see the Louvre's most famous lady… the Mona Lisa. I'm afraid the only thing they'll be able on a day like today is the head of the person in front of them. If you want to visit the Mona Lisa, you need to come on a winter evening. You'll be alone with her."

For a brief instant, Ava almost wished it were winter so she could experience that intimacy. But the sunlight streaming through the window changed her mind. It was summer. If she had her way, the beautiful weather would last forever.

"When did you last see the Mona Lisa?" Henri asked.

"I can't remember." No sooner had the words escaped her lips than a school trip to the Louvre years ago came to mind. At the time, Ava, who must have been fourteen, had been more interested in a boy called Jason than in art. She had a vague memory of standing in front of the Mona Lisa as he chatted up another girl, breaking Ava's heart.

"The Mona Lisa is a wonderful painting, but it's far from my favorite," Henri said.

"What are we seeing today?" Ava asked, taking another forkful of her apple tart. She was so ravenous, she considered picking it up with her fingers and biting into it. She refrained from doing so. Certain things were not done in France.

"13ᵗʰ and 14ᵗʰ century Italian painting," Henri said. "We'll see works by Lorenzo Monaco, Bartolo di Fredi and Pisanello. Pisanello's portrait of the Princess of Este is enchanting." Gazing at the mass of people walking up the staircase, he shook his head. "Don't worry. We'll be far from the maddening crowd."

"I remember visiting museums on school trips. We were shepherded past painting after painting without having the chance to look at any of them. Angels and saints, sinners and sinking ships… they all blended into one big blur," Ava said, twirling her fork in the air.

Henri grinned. "I prefer sinners. Saints are never much fun."

"Uncle Charles would have agreed with you. He liked rogues and villains. I think he'd be disappointed in me."

Henri burst out laughing. "You're still young. There's plenty of time to pick up vices."

Finding his words encouraging, Ava finished her tart. "Cheesecake and apple tart aren't very French for breakfast."

"All the better. If you believed the clichés, I'd have a beret on my head, and you'd have bright pink hair. Besides, this is a late breakfast. It doesn't follow the normal Parisian breakfast rules."

Ava studied Henri as he drank his espresso. He was at home in the ostentatious gold and marble surroundings. Henri was a former French *notaire*, a notary. In France, a notary was a member of a powerful caste. They were wealthy, secretive and protective of privileges that went back hundreds of years.

Henri had once joked to Ava, "Not only do we know where the bodies are buried, we buried them… if we didn't kill the people ourselves."

A French notary giving up his practice before he was in his dotage or dead was as rare as Christmas in August…

Impossible.

However, Henri was Christmas in August.

And also in May, June and July.

In short, Henri was an unusual man.

He had come to Paris from Bordeaux -- a city in southwestern France, hub of the Bordeaux wine-growing region -- to deal with a tricky inheritance. Her Uncle Charles's apartment where she now lived had sprung from that, as had the book stands and Henri's country house in the middle of Paris.

At a mere sixty, Henri had sold his practice to his nephew and moved to Paris. Henri's former clients still appeared on a regular basis to ask him for advice. But after a long leisurely lunch at Café Zola, they would leave, reassured.

To Ava, it seemed that if anyone lived life fully, it was Henri. He truly enjoyed people. He loved food, knowledge and beauty. He had a great sense of humor and had been a true friend to her since she had moved to Paris to become a bookseller.

And after they had saved Yves Dubois, a university professor, from being murdered, she and Henri were now partners in sleuthing.

"*Sext and DeAth*. It has a nice ring to it, doesn't it?" Ava asked.

"Are you having a sign made?" Henri asked, smiling.

"Of course not. I just find it curious that you and my uncle became friends. Knowing him, he would have found the wordplay on your names extremely funny."

Henri grinned. "I agree. Charles liked the ring of *Sext and*

DeAth."

Ava nodded. Henri's last name was often a source of astonishment for English speakers. DeAth was an old Flemish name. *De* meant from. *Ath* was a city in Belgium. Over time, the pronunciation of the last name had come to rhyme with the English word "death". As both her uncle and Henri possessed a wicked sense of humor, Ava suspected their last names had made their friendship inevitable.

Thinking of her uncle, Ava glanced away to hide the tears in her eyes. She owed her Paris life to him. In his will, he had left her an apartment and money. More importantly, he had left her Henri.

Looking around, Ava noticed that the café was now half-full.

When had everyone snuck in?

When she and Henri had arrived, the café had been empty.

Her Uncle Charles had often said that people miss half their lives because they don't see what's going on around them. Ava might not have missed half her life, but she had certainly missed the last ten minutes.

All at once, a shadow loomed over her.

A tall man in his late forties with wavy brown hair and blue eyes, even bluer than Henris, was standing next to her. He seemed relieved to see her. As his eyes ran over her face, his expression changed. Confused, he looked up and peered out the window.

Startled, Ava eyed the man, waiting. French people didn't walk up to strangers unless it was urgent.

"It's a beautiful day, isn't it?" the man asked in a posh English accent.

The moment Ava heard his accent, she smiled. The man was not a desperate Frenchman. He was a fellow compatriot who had fallen under the city's spell.

"June is a lovely month to visit Paris," Henri said.

The man eyed Henri. "Do we know one another?"

"I don't believe so. I'm Henri DeAth." Henri gestured at Ava. "My friend is Ava Sext."

The man smiled. "I'm George Starr."

"Are you here on a visit?" Henri asked in a breezy tone.

"No. I'm lucky enough to live here," George said with a grin. He turned his head to the right. Instantly, his body became rigid. Turning white, he stepped back as if warding off a blow.

Noticing the dramatic change in the man's behavior, Ava glanced around to see what had caused it. All she saw was a sea of shouting French schoolchildren being corralled through the café to the outside terrace by their teachers.

And then, like in a film, everything happened at once.

Or so it seemed to Ava.

George tilted forward and fell over the table. "Sorry. How clumsy of me," he said as he pulled himself up, clutching the chair next to her.

Before Ava could respond, George turned and sprinted out of the café, pushing his way through the rambunctious children.

Alarmed, Ava jumped up. "Henri! Something's wrong!"

Having sensed that something was off, Henri was already on his feet.

"He's headed to the stairs, Henri!" Ava shouted as she ran to the black and gold wrought iron railing that overlooked the stairway. When she reached it, there was a loud, ear-shattering scream.

The scream echoed through the café.

In horror, Ava glanced down and saw George Starr fly up in the air and go bouncing down the stone stairs. His body hit the landing with a loud thud.

For a moment, time stopped.

Everyone was silent.

No one moved.

Then sheer chaos ensued.

Screams and shouts of horror rang up from the stairwell.

Ava started to run toward the stairs. Henri held her back.

The screams and shouts were now coming from all around them. Everyone in the café leapt up and ran to the railing to see what had happened.

Feeling sick, Ava pressed her back against a stone pillar and looked down at George. His body was sprawled on the stone landing. His head was at an odd angle, and blood dripped from the back of his skull. There was no question of whether he was dead or alive.

No one could have survived a fall like that.

With a solemn look on his face, Henri turned to Ava. "I suggest we postpone our museum visit."

Frozen to the spot, Ava stared down at the body of the man who had been chatting gaily with her seconds before.

In a flash, Ava knew that the death was not an accident. For some unknown reason, George Starr had been murdered. Looking down at his lifeless body, Ava vowed to discover who the murderer was.

ABOUT THE BOOKS

Evan's *Paris Booksellers Mysteries* plunge into the joys and tribulations of living in Paris, where food, wine and crime make life worth living… along with a book or two.

She also writes the *Isa Floris* thrillers that blend together far-flung locations, ancient secrets and fast-paced action in an intriguing mix of fact and fiction aimed at keeping you on the edge of your seat.

Find out more about Evan Hirst's books at

www.evanhirst.com

SCDR2000001121B
TYPE C DRIVE SCREEN .18

Made in the USA
Middletown, DE
11 December 2019